Also by R. Scott Mackey

Ray Courage Mystery Series

Courage Begins: A Ray Courage Mystery Novella

Courage Matters

Non-fiction

Barbary Baseball: The Pacific Coast League of the 1920s

COURAGE
RESURRECTED

A novel by R. Scott Mackey

Big Hound Publishing
Sacramento, CA

For Mariah

Prologue

Pam Courage drove and drove and drove, a brilliant November mid-afternoon turning to dusk then dark. She made the same loop four times. Sacramento to Davis and back again. She'd driven more than two hundred miles, but clarity would not come. She usually thought best when she drove alone. Today, not so much.

How had everything become so screwed up so quickly? This was not a gradual buildup of events, or a perfect storm of random happenings, nothing that she could have predicted or seen coming. This was a two-ton anvil falling out of the sky and clobbering her. The meeting with Yuri had been a disaster. Ray? He'd upset her like never before.

Her cell phone rang on the passenger seat. Ray. Now the third time he had called, no doubt worried, maybe approaching frantic as the dinner hour had come and long since passed. No, let it go to voice mail. Ray. God dammit.

More than five hours had passed since she had surprised Dr. Susan Whitehead when she dropped in to her office unannounced. Pam had never been to a psychologist before, but Dr. Whitehead had helped others in her office. They talked only briefly, Pam too distracted to say much more than she'd fought with her husband in the morning, and problems at work had her distressed. Dr. Whitehead had encouraged her to talk more. Instead, Pam said she needed to think things through

1

on her own. So she drove.

She would have to go home. She could not keep driving, avoiding the inevitable. No, this time she would merge onto Interstate 5 and go home. She owed it to herself and she owed it to Ray.

Just a couple of days ago she considered her life almost perfect. Great job. A good marriage. She thought about Sara and the joy she felt when she watched her daughter play tennis and soccer. Now she had the lead in the sixth grade play. A budding thespian. Was there anything that her twelve-year old daughter couldn't do? Pam had been the same way as a girl. Confident. Adventurous. Fearless. She smiled. Quickly the smile evaporated. Now here she was, her confidence shaken to its very core, everything she felt true and right turned upside down. Not in a million years would she have predicted this happening to her. She looked at her eyes in the rearview mirror and saw something almost animalistic—panic, fear and hopelessness.

Her hands on the steering wheel did not obey the direction from her weakening will as she flew past Sutterville Road, the exit leading home. Five miles later she exited at Meadowview Road, turned right on to Freeport Boulevard and drove past the tiny town of Freeport, where the road met the river and followed its windy route towards the delta. Here there were no streetlights, nothing but darkness and the narrow tunnel of illumination from her headlights.

The cell phone rang again.

"Shit." Even without looking at it she knew it was Ray. But this time, rather than spurring her to drive on, the call convinced her to return home. Her grumbling stomach announced the hunger she'd been ignoring all afternoon.

She never drove down here, by the river, where she regularly read of cars plunging off the side into the cold waters, the bodies of drivers, passengers, men, women and children fished out by grim scuba divers. Though only ten miles from home, she felt in another world, a million miles away. A dark place, timeless, untouched by civilization. She turned up the heater to combat the increasing chill of the late fall evening.

She glanced in the rearview mirror again and noticed a truck following a couple of hundred feet back, its headlight higher and farther apart than those of a car. Had there been someone behind her when she started her aimless journey? Of course there had. She had been driving on some of the most traveled freeways and roads in Northern California, millions of vehicles passed over them each day. At any given moment there was sure to be someone—a car or a truck— right behind her. She'd been so lost in her thoughts all day that she never paused to think about the other cars around her; yet her subconscious seemed to have been at work because it told her that the truck behind her right now, shrouded in the black night, had been with her all day. She snorted at the idea and its improbability. She was getting tired and starting to imagine things.

Cold, hungry, and growing more afraid in the alien landscape, she looked for a side road or pullout so that she could turn around. About mile later she spotted the driveway leading to a house on the right side of the road. She slowed and flicked on her blinker. The truck behind her seemed to slow as well.

A wrought iron gate guarded the driveway, but there was enough space between it and the road for Pam to pull over and turn back towards the road at a ninety-degree angle. She looked to her right to make sure the lane heading back towards Sacramento was clear. She looked left to see the vehicle advancing on her. Advancing *at* her, its high beams blinding.

She reached down for the shifter to put it into reverse, but failed to engage the release button, leaving her car centered in the road. The truck was going to hit her. With little choice, she floored the accelerator to propel herself forward and out of harm's way. The truck veered towards her new path.

Walter Heffner told police that night that he thought an airliner had crashed on the road in front of his house, the sound so deafening, the eruption of flames so huge that only an object that large moving that fast could explain it. By the time he put on his shoes and coat he saw what was left of a car straddling the center stripe of the two-lane country road, the heat from the fire so great that he could not get within a hundred feet. His eyes searched the now brightly lit landscape for a second vehicle or whatever might have caused such a conflagration. He looked up the road and down. Nothing but darkness. That seemed strange to him.

Thirteen Years Later
November 11

one

"Why should I believe that you've changed?" Rubia asked the thick Hispanic man with the neck tattoos. She studied him, awaiting his response.

The man's eyes moved slowly up from the table to look at her. "It changes you," he said softly, putting his hand over his heart. "Ten years in prison can make you go one of two ways. You can either let it make you even harder. Or, you can choose to change, to be better, to walk away from the brutality all around you."

To me, an ex-college professor turned private investigator, this man seemed sincere. I knew Rubia, who had grown up on the streets, in a world so much different from mine, might see him differently. I watched my former student to see how she would react.

The three of us sat at a small table inside the cramped offices of It's My Life, or IML as it was usually called, the non-profit Rubia had founded after she quit running one of the most ruthless gangs in West Sacramento. By the time she had enrolled in my organizational communication class at Sacramento State University, two busts and a dozen tattoos later, she had gone straight. Then, as now, it was difficult for me to imagine this beautiful, petite Latina with the sad brown eyes and long black hair to be an ex-gangbanger. She possessed the street smarts, guile, and viciousness to run Los Modernos, the gang that ran

4

the largest meth operation in the north state. IML's goal was to steer kids away from gang life by focusing on school, sports, and other more productive activities. I had agreed to volunteer a few hours a week to help her, though I felt woefully inadequate for the task. Even here, interviewing a possible employee, I lacked the experience to know what would pass for street cred with teen and pre-teen kids in the poor, drug riddled streets of Sacramento. Ray Courage, clueless, middle-aged white guy.

"I will get back to you on your cell," Rubia said after a long pause during which she appeared to battle her thoughts about Edgar Ruiz.

"Just so you know, I'll take any pay, even minimum wage. For me it's not about the money. I need to do what's right and this is a place where I can make a difference."

"Okay, Edgar, let me think about it for a day."

"Thank you."

After he left, I asked if she was going to hire him.

"Not sure. He might work out. Seems like he's turned it around. I can relate to what he said about how you can go one of two directions once you're inside. That's exactly what I went through. So, he might be the right guy for the job."

"You said that about the last two guys, the one who died from an overdose and the one who's now back at Folsom Prison for murder."

"Thank you, Little Mister Sunshine."

My cell phone vibrated in my pocket to announce the arrival of an e-mail. I pulled out my phone and glanced at the subject and the sender: "You need to read this" from Pam1111@blazermail.com. Probably junk mail. I returned the phone to my pocket. My thoughts drifted back and, reflexively, I sighed.

"Ray, are you going to tell me what's going on with you?" Rubia asked.

"It's November," I said, finally answering truthfully the question she'd been asking all week. "I always get this way in November."

"Pam."

I nodded. November no longer brought tears, those had stopped a few years ago. It did bring heartache and memories, though usually good memories after so long. I couldn't help but miss her, now thirteen years ago to this day, November 11, when she died in a horrific automobile accident. I missed so much about her—our bike rides in the park, laughing at the same stupid sitcoms, having a cup of coffee while we read the morning paper together, and mainly the time spent together with our daughter Sara. We were a close family, watching our daughter's tennis matches and soccer games, our weekends consumed by her activities. We didn't mind that at all. Mind it? Hell, we lived for it. Some of the other parents complained that they had no lives because of all the things they did for their children. Not us. We loved every minute of it. Sure, maybe it seemed like everything centered on Sara, but it brought all of us closer, sharing those times together. After the accident, when it was just my daughter and me, things became so different. Sara and I grew even closer, that closeness partially filling the void left by losing Pam.

"Get over it Ray. We've got too much shit to do here."

Rubia. I appreciated that so much more than all the clichéd condolences everyone else offered. We worked for another hour, she making calls to set up meetings with a half dozen kids the following week while I created a spreadsheet of schools and contacts where we hoped to make presentations about IML.

"All right, I'm out of here," she announced just after six o'clock. "I've got a hot date tonight so I need some time to get pretty."

"What's that involve, deciding which tattoos to reveal?"

"Ha, ha."

After she left I took out my phone and opened the email from Pam1111, fully intending to delete it after a quick glance. Instead of some offer for an erection booster or the chance to aid a Nigerian princess, the message gave me an immediate chill:

> *Ray,*
> *How could you have done that to me 13 years ago?*
> *Me, the person you said you loved? Well, it didn't*
> *work. I'm not dead and I am going to make you pay*
> *after all these years. Better look over your shoulder.*
> *Pam*

Who could be so cruel to send me a message like this? Pam1111. My wife's name and the day she died. November 11. The sender knew that today was the thirteenth anniversary of her death. Who disliked me so much that they would try to hurt me by sending such a cruel message? Only a few names came to mind and they didn't fit. Lionel Stroud, my previous client. He and I had a few run-ins but in the end we parted without any lingering resentment. No, it wasn't Stroud.

Then there was the young woman, the student, who accused me of sexual harassment when I was still teaching at Sacramento State. The subsequent investigation deemed her charges spurious and she left the university disgraced. A few months later I left as well, unable to deal with the sideways glances and whispers when I approached a group of students or fellow professors. An exonerated man, but guilty in the court of public opinion solely on the basis of a false accusation. No, she didn't seem likely either. Both she and I paid for her lie, and it could be argued mine came at the steeper price. She seemed an unlikely suspect at best.

And what about the content of the message? It was bad enough that the sender tried to trick me into thinking Pam still lived. To suggest that I had been the one who killed her—or tried to kill her—went beyond cruel, the stuff of a deviant, someone who'd pull the wings off flies, lacerate cats, and torment widowers with false accusations of attempted murder.

I concluded the e-mail had been sent by a prankster. A mean-spirited prankster, but a prankster nonetheless. My finger hovered over the delete icon. I pulled it back and let the message stay, just in case.

A much-needed rain began to fall, the heavy drops plinking the top of my car as I approached it from the IML office. It hadn't rained this hard in a couple of years. Many of us in California wondered if the three-year drought had become the new normal, one of the consequences of global warming. Watching it through the window of my car made me feel good, as if the drought might be one less thing I'd have to worry about. My mind had already shifted from the e-mail to what to have for dinner when my cell phone vibrated again.

The muscles in my test tightened when I saw the message came from Pam1111. I opened it.

7

The body of the e-mail was blank, the message contained only an attachment. I debated the wisdom of opening the PDF labeled only "article," but my curiosity overcame my fear of infecting my phone with a virus. The *Sacramento Bee* article from thirteen years before recounted the fiery car accident that had killed my wife. At the bottom of the article someone had scrawled in ink:

> *Nice try, Ray.*
> *Pam*

My giddiness about the rain suddenly evaporated.

two

The rain did not ease up on the drive across the bridge from West Sacramento to Sacramento. The steady downpour had me white-knuckled enough behind the wheel. Adding in the messages in the two e-mails and I had a full spook on. By the time I pulled into my driveway, the evening and my house were pitch-dark. I paused before inserting my key in the front door. Could somebody—the person who'd sent the two messages that could only be categorized as threatening—be waiting for me inside?

I stood on the porch a good thirty seconds before convincing myself to unlock the door and walk inside. No one assaulted me or said "boo." I didn't immediately see any notes or portends of violence. I certainly didn't see Pam standing in my living room. I exhaled and went to the kitchen.

Lately I'd been doing a better job of grocery shopping so that I had enough food and ingredients on hand to make myself decent dinners. Living alone as I did, cooking offered a pleasurable activity in the evenings. That morning I placed my recipe for Mexican bean soup on the kitchen counter. Soup weather had clearly arrived and I wanted to make something that would last for a couple of dinners and a couple of lunches. This recipe filled the bill.

I started prepping the meal the way I always did—by cracking open a bottle of beer, this one a Panic IPA from Sacramento's own Track 7 Brewing Company. Just like seemingly every city in the United States, Sacramento had gone craft-beer-crazy, a welcome phenomena for an inveterate beer drinker like me. Once I filled my pint glass, I started chopping an onion, pausing several times to let the inevitable tears clear out. Next, I chopped four cloves of garlic and diced four pounds of pork. I put all of that in a large stockpot with oil for browning. The Panic IPA tasted great, the first time I had tried this particular beer from Track 7. To the onions, garlic, and pork I added chili powder, oregano, cumin, water, beef broth, and pinto beans. I'd let that simmer for a couple of hours before adding carrots and pickled baby corncobs. It would be a late dinner but worth the wait.

While the soup simmered, I retrieved my cell phone from the kitchen table and hit speed dial.

"Hi Dad," Sara said, answering after just two rings.

"Hey, did I catch you at a good time?"

"Of course. It's always a good time for you."

"Wow! I'm flattered. Christmas must be coming up."

"You saw right through me," she said.

"I just called to see how things are going? How's law school?"

"I can't wait for the semester to be over. But other than that everything is fine."

A silence ensued as I missed the cue to continue my part of the conversation.

"Dad?"

"Yeah."

"Are you okay?"

"Yeah, sure, fine. Why not?"

"Because I know what day it is."

I should have figured Sara would remember November 11, even after all these years, even after going to class all day four hundred miles away. I guess you never forget the day you lost your mom.

"You'd think it would get easier as the years go by," I said. "It doesn't."

Sara sighed. "Did you go to the … did you go visit her today?"

"Yes, in the morning, before it rained." Pam's cremated remains were buried up in Auburn, near where her parents lived, about an hour away in the foothills.

"I wish I could be there with you today."

10

"I wish you could, too," I said.

"You know, for me every year it gets harder to remember her. I feel guilty about that. I mean I remember lots of thing, especially some of the big things like our trips together, some of our Christmases. Things like that. I've forgotten some of the little stuff, though. Like the mornings before school, what we did around the dinner table. You know, the day in and day out things. I have these vague images of everyday life with Mom, but nothing concrete anymore."

"You were only twelve when you lost her. It was a long time ago. Over half your life ago."

"I just feel like I should remember more. It seems like losing memories of her makes it like she's dying all over again. Makes me sad."

"Maybe I shouldn't have called."

"No, it's nothing you did. And November 11 will always be a day I think about her."

I wanted to change the subject, if only slightly, to the reason I had called. "Did anything unusual happen today?"

"Unusual? What do you mean?"

I had clumsily blundered onto the subject. I didn't want to alarm her, though I needed to find out if the wacko who'd been bothering me today had reached out to her as well. "I don't know, anything about your mom or me?"

"I still don't understand. What about mom or you?"

I paused. "Did you get an e-mail or anything else about either of us?"

"No. Why would I?"

I told her about the e-mails I'd received from Pam1111, though I was vague about the content, summarizing the message as coming from an unnamed person and that included speculation that Pam's car crash was not accidental. I didn't mention that the writer claimed to be Pam, who was accusing me of attempted murder.

"That's weird," she said.

"Can you read me the e-mails?"

"I already deleted them," I lied. "They're just pranks."

"Should you call the police?"

"No, it's just some wack job with nothing better to do. I just wanted to make sure that they haven't been bothering you, too. That's all."

"I'm fine. But I do think you should let somebody know about it."

"I'll think it over," I said, ending the topic. We chatted for a few more minutes about school and our upcoming holiday plans before we said our goodbyes.

Back in the kitchen, I diced up four cups of carrots, retrieved the jar of baby corncobs and set it on the counter. I poured the rest of the beer into my glass and headed for the living room to see if the game was on television. The Kings were playing the Lakers. I had just found the channel carrying the game when the doorbell rang. Only people asking for money came to my door, that they would do so at eight o'clock particularly annoyed me. I decided not to answer. The doorbell rang a second time, then a third.

Ticked off, I stomped to the door and flung it open. Before I could unleash the torrent of words I had in my head, a rotund woman in a raincoat stuck a badge in my face.

"Detective Carla Thurber, Sac PD," she said. "Are you Raymond Courage?"

Could my day get any weirder? "Yes. Why?"

"Do you mind if I come in. It's cold and wet out here."

I stepped back and let her in. She took off her raincoat and I pointed to the rack in the entry where she could hang it. She was middle-aged, probably younger than I, stood maybe five-five, though her weight pushed two hundred pounds. Her round face was topped with short, mousy brown hair. She wore no makeup or lipstick.

"What can I do for you?" I said as we stood in the entry. I had no idea why this detective stood here in my home. In my previous case, my encounters with a Sac PD lieutenant named Nick Trujillo were, shall we say, less than positive. Detective Thurber's demeanor and comportment thus far gave little reason for me to expect a better experience with her.

"Can we sit down?"

"Is this going to take so long that we need to sit down?"

"Yes," she said, curtly.

12

We settled into the living room. I lowered the sound of the television, though I left the game on. Once I set down the remote I drank some of my beer.

"I can see that you're busy so I'll get right to the point," Thurber said as I drank. "I received a phone call this afternoon about the accident several years ago involving your wife."

I could feel the color drain from my face. What in the hell was going on? "Go on," I managed to say.

"First of all, do you know anything about that?"

"The phone call or my wife's accident?" For once I wasn't trying to be a smartass; I really didn't know what she meant.

"The phone call."

"No. Who was the call from?"

"You know nothing about a phone call, then?"

"I said I didn't."

"All right then. The caller was a woman, or at least sounded like a woman. She said that she had evidence that your wife's accident was not an accident. That someone deliberately killed her."

"What? Did this person tell you her name?"

"She did not."

"Then you can track her down from her phone."

Thurber shook her head. "Throwaway phone. Couldn't track it to anybody other than the Target store on Broadway, where the person paid cash for the phone."

"So some crank call about a thirteen-year-old car accident has you out working at eight o'clock at night in a pouring rain?" Much as I dreaded hearing it, I knew that she had more.

"Like I said, this caller said that she had proof. When I asked her what that was, she said she would deliver it in due time. For now, she just asked that I at least look at the case file. So, just to amuse myself, I did that. Spent a good hour reviewing the official report."

"And?"

"And your wife's accident does look suspicious. Very suspicious."

"Come on!" I blurted out. "My wife died in a car accident thirteen years ago. It was thoroughly investigated at the time, not just by the street cops but they even brought in a detective as I remember. I forget his name, but—"

"Lewis. Detective Lewis."

"Okay. He looked into it and concluded that Pam died in an accidental car crash." I noticed that she was studying me as I spoke and didn't like what that implied. Any temptation that I had to tell her about the e-mails vanished then and there.

"He did, indeed," she said slowly, once she was sure I was done speaking. "You see I knew Detective Lewis. He was one of my first partners in the department. I don't like to speak ill of anyone, but Lewis was not a good cop. Lazy. Worried more about where we were going to have lunch than conducting a proper investigation. He retired years ago and his investigation of your wife's accident was one of his last cases. When I saw his name in the case file, it caught my attention."

"What did you find in the file?" I asked. Something had prompted her to come see me unannounced, besides the fact Lewis was a lazy cop.

"For one, the lack of a second vehicle in the accident. Clearly, Pamela's car struck something big and solid in the middle of that road. Struck it so hard that it should have been in as bad a shape as her car, which was a freaking mess. His report didn't account for that other than to say the other vehicle drove away."

"I already know this. Lewis shared it with me. He said the other vehicle must have been larger, like a truck or something, and left the scene for whatever reason."

"For whatever reason, yeah." She looked me in the eyes for several seconds.

"Go on," I said, maintaining my eye contact with her.

"Pamela's car caught fire very quickly, unusually so. And according to the first eyewitness on the scene who lived in the nearby house, by the time he reached the road—maybe two minutes after the accident—the car was completely ablaze. It was as if someone had doused the entire vehicle with gasoline or some other accelerant and then torched it."

"They said the gas tank probably exploded," I said. "Wouldn't that account for it?"

"Probably not. Gas tanks don't explode as easily as people think.

14

Your wife drove a hybrid that carried, at most, ten gallons of gas. Lewis didn't check your wife's old credit card records to see when she last filled up the car, but I did. It had been almost a week. My guess is there was less than half a tank in that car when it was hit."

"Five gallons could start a pretty good fire," I said, immediately regretting it, sounding like I was defending Lewis and not caring that my wife could have been killed deliberately.

"Maybe. Probably not, though. Also, in this case it's likely that the extreme impact severed the fuel line, pierced the tank, or blew off the gas cap. Any one of those things would have depressurized the tank making an explosion highly unlikely. Sure, leaking gas and any flame present could have caused the fire to spread. But the speed and magnitude of the blaze was atypical. I would have called it suspicious."

"I don't know what to tell you. I trusted the investigation at the time. The way you put it does make it sound suspicious, but what can we do now? Wait a second, you said this anonymous caller had proof. What kind of proof?"

"She didn't really say. Like I told you, she said she'd provide it when she was ready to do so. She did say that you and your wife had a terrible fight that morning. Is that true?"

"No." I hoped I sounded convincing.

"From the case file it doesn't sound like Detective Lewis asked where you were at the time of accident, let alone look for corroborating witnesses. Again, very lazy."

"Wait a minute, are you suggesting I killed my wife because we had an argument?"

"Not suggesting anything. Just noticing a lot of problems with the investigation is all. The caller suggested you caused the accident."

"This is just beyond bizarre," I said. "You can't possibly think—"

"I'm just telling you what the caller said, that's all."

"Are you planning to reopen the case?"

"Thinking about it. Since we've already opened the subject, I do want to ask you where you were on the night of your wife's death."

"Home."

"Anyone see or talk to you at the time"

"Look, Thurber, this line of questioning is not going to happen. I

15

am not going to be insulted by you. If you want to go on this witch hunt, then you'd better look somewhere else."

Thurber stared at me several seconds before a tight smile remained on her face as she stood, retrieved her coat, and opened the front door.

"I'll be in touch," she said before she left. "Very soon."

November 12

three

By five the next morning I gave up on trying to sleep. After showering, I brewed a quarter pot of coffee, made myself an egg and cheese sandwich, and settled in with that morning's *Sacramento Bee*, half expecting to see a headline along the lines of "Husband charged in thirteen-year-old murder of wife" accompanied by a photo of yours truly sneering into the camera. By the time I finished breakfast and confirmed that I had not been featured in the newspaper, I set out for Clarksburg.

During the drive, I recounted for the umpteenth time the conversation with Carla Thurber the night before. Whoever was messing with me was mixing up story lines. To me, my unknown accuser claimed to be Pam and still alive. To Thurber, she claimed to be a witness, or at least someone who had evidence, linking me to Pam's murder. Was there any significance to this? Or was the difference simply a result of this person's instability and irrationality?

I arrived at my destination about six-fifty in the morning, just as the sun inched its way above the Sacramento River. A pullout about fifty yards past the spot afforded enough room to park the car and walk along the road upstream to the spot where Pam had died. The last time I was here was the day after the accident. Even then I didn't know why I did that, though I suspect it was partly denial that Pam had really died. I needed to see the physical place where it happened, to see the scorched cement and the fragments of her car that remained after the police did their work and hauled the wreckage away. Now, as then, I didn't feel anything special about this place, not a mystical connection or a revulsion, nothing other than a sense of life's fragility, that our death can come any time, any place. Even here, on a straight stretch of road near Clarksburg.

A straight stretch of road. That nagged at me. Looking up the road in the direction from which the vehicle that hit Pam had come, I could see for a good two hundred yards, maybe more. Even on a dark and rainy night, as on the night of the accident, a driver could see well enough to avoid barreling into a car on the side of the road with its lights on. Of course, the driver could have been impaired by drugs, alcohol, or a medical condition. Yet that straight shot of road bugged me. It at least raised the possibility that someone had deliberately collided with my wife's car as she waited to make a U-turn, as the police speculated she'd been doing.

The entrance to the driveway where I now stood led to the house of the first witness to the accident, or to the aftermath of the accident, because, by the time he arrived, the car had already erupted into flames. Heffner. Walter Heffner was the man's name. He was in his seventies back then. I wondered if he might still be alive and living here. I tried to open the gate but it was locked. No lights were on at the house some fifty yards away. Probably not a good idea to visit unannounced at seven in the morning anyway.

It was too early to start on the work I needed to do for my insurance company client, so I drove around the tiny town of Clarksburg. Except for a general store, which was closed at this early hour, I didn't see any commercial establishments at all. Some of the houses in the four blocks I drove were coming to life, and a couple of early arriving teachers were pulling into the parking lot at Clarksburg High School.

Back on River Road, I headed towards Sacramento, crossed the bridge that put me back on the east side of the river, passed by a golf course, then pulled into the parking lot of the Freeport Grill.

Even at this early hour, three men sat at the bar drinking beer. From their dress—jeans, flannel shirts, and ball caps—they appeared to be fishermen, likely owners of the small boat attached to the pickup truck I noticed in the parking lot. I settled onto a stool at the far end of the bar, a couple of empty seats between me and the three men. The bartender, a petite Asian woman of about thirty, placed a paper coaster in front of me. I ordered a cup of coffee. When she returned we exchanged pleasantries and I asked if she lived in the area.

"My whole life. Three generations of Kubos were born and raised here in Freeport."

"Like it?"

"Yeah, I guess so. Kind of the best of both worlds, really. Small town where you get to know everybody and everything's kind of relaxed. Then, less than three miles up the road, you have the big city. It's cool. What about you? Where are you from?"

"Sacramento. Lived there over twenty years." I sipped the coffee.

"What brings you down here?" She was pretty, on the short side with silky black hair that fell to the middle of her back. Her attire fit the establishment, casual and comfortable, blue jeans and a plain white T-shirt with "Freeport Grill" printed in blue letters across the chest.

"Just wanted to get out of the city and go for a drive." I saw no reason to mention the real reason.

"It's a nice day for a drive. But you need to be careful driving the River Road in the winter. Not enough guard rails on the river's side of the road. I bet I've heard of twenty cars in my life sliding off the road and into the water. Hardly any of them make it out."

She moved over to the fishermen, who tried to decide whether to order another round or to venture out to the water. They eventually opted to settle their tab and head out, leaving the bar to the bartender and me. She finished clearing the glasses and wiping down the bar where the men had sat before grabbing the coffee pot to freshen my cup.

"You've lived here your whole life," I said as she poured. "Do you remember a few years ago when a car crashed and burst into flames near Clarksburg?"

"I do," she said, returning the pot to the burner on the back of the

19

bar before resuming the conversation. "I was in high school and I remember everybody talking about it because it was a big deal for this area. You could see that fire all the way from here. Then all the fire trucks, cops, the whole nine yards. It was a big scene. Long time ago, though."

"What did people think about it at the time? You know, the fact they never found the second vehicle in the crash?"

She laughed. "Like I said, I was in high school. We talked about all kinds of crazy shit. You know, things like the driver ran into Big Foot, or it was a UFO that did it. Things kids would say."

"Yeah, I can imagine." I thought about my students back when I was teaching at Sac State. Some of the things they thought and believed never failed to amaze me. "Were there rumors or anything besides *National Enquirer* stuff?"

She thought about that for a second, then nodded. "Come to think of it, for a few days we did think that maybe this guy who lives down in Locke might have done it."

"Why did this particular guy get singled out in the rumor mill?"

"The guy's name was Larry Slager. He was like fifty years old back then. The family was kind of prominent in the area. His dad had been a farmer and made a ton of money. Larry didn't have the brains of his dad. Plus he was an ornery drunk. Almost every day he'd drink at some hole in the wall in West Sac then drive the River Road home dead drunk. That's something like thirty miles on a winding dark road. Our parents always used to warn us—we were teenagers, most with brand new driver's licenses—to be on the lookout for him on the road. If we saw him we were supposed to stay the hell out of his way."

I thought about the possibility of Larry Slager killing my wife. Kind of a stretch. "Do you know if the police ever talked to him?"

She shrugged. "Dunno. How come you're so interested in this car accident, anyway? It was so long ago."

"Driving around down here just brought it to mind and I started wondering if anything came of it. Does this Slager still live in Locke?"

"I think so. I know his company is still there, so he probably is, too."

"He's a farmer?"

"No, he's in the towing business. Not like auto association towing. They tow big rigs. Been doing that for twenty years. He's got this fleet of big-ass tow trucks the size of small houses. That was another reason our parents told us to steer clear of him, because he'd didn't drive home drunk in a car or pickup truck like everybody else drove. Nope. He always drove one of those big old trucks home. If one of us crashed into him we would have been smashed like a bug."

She loaded some dirty glasses in the under-bar dishwasher before leaving the bar area for a couple of minutes, returning with a case of Budweiser. She knelt down and began loading a bottle at a time into a refrigerator at the back of the bar under the cash register.

"Do you know anything about Walter Heffner?" I said.

"Sure, everybody knows Walter."

"I guess everybody knows everybody around here."

"Pretty much," she said, standing back up after finishing with the case of beer.

"I was thinking about talking to him about the accident. He was the only witness."

"I wouldn't waste your time," she said. "Old Walter, bless his heart, his attic's a little dusty."

"Excuse me?"

"Dementia. He still lives at the house but he has a full-time caregiver. Walter thinks he's back fighting the Korean War."

I let the conversation end there and finished my coffee. Before I stood up from the barstool another thought crowded in with my mental note to find this Slager guy, the same thought that had finally rousted me from bed a few hours earlier. Only Pam and I knew we fought that morning. Sara was at school. It had been a bitter fight, the worst in our marriage by far.

How could anyone else have known? Only one answer came to mind, an answer that chilled my heart. Pam was alive.

21

four

I let myself into the Say Hey bar shortly after eleven in the morning, about an hour before Rubia normally opened the place. Deciding to leave the front door unlocked in case any early customers arrived, I flicked on the lights, started a pot of coffee, settled in at a corner table, and started my laptop.

Rubia inherited the Say Hey from her uncle, a sports photographer for the *Bee*, who, during his career, managed to shoot and collect a total of four hundred fifty-three photos of Willie ("The Say Hey Kid") Mays, all of them adorning the walls of the bar that now served as a shrine to the great baseball player. Considering that the Say Hey covered maybe five hundred square feet, the photos covered nearly every available inch of the walls. The collection attracted baseball and photography fans from near and far. Rubia said her uncle once turned down fifty thousand dollars for all of them.

The first video file I opened on my laptop showed the subject of my insurance investigation working on his cabin in Graegle. The man moved a stack of two-by-fours from his driveway into the partially constructed interior of the cabin. He then climbed a ladder and made some tape measurements before spending a half hour cutting the two-by-fours into different lengths. Physical work for a county maintenance worker claiming a one hundred percent disability for a bad back. I shot the video last week and needed to put it together with my report for the insurance company and their attorney before the man's workers' comp hearing next week. This guy was gonna be toast.

"Hey, professor, what's up?" Rubia seemed cheery, not a mood she exhibited often.

"You seem particularly ebullient today."

"Ebullient. I like it when you talk like a professor. Gets me all tingly."

"And I'm just warming up. So why the good mood?"

"Good date last night," she said.

"Anything you'd like to share?"

"Wouldn't want to embarrass you and your middle-class sensibilities."

"Good to know you're looking out for me."

She began prepping the bar, cutting up lime slices, skinning and cutting lemons into twist-sized lengths, filling trays with olives and Maraschino cherries, and putting celery stalks into a water glass in anticipation of an early afternoon run on Bloody Marys. "Can you stick around for awhile?"

"Why?" I asked.

"I've got another guy coming in for an IML interview. Called me this morning and said a friend told him about the gig."

"Sure. I don't know how helpful I'm going to be, though. I didn't say jack to Edgar yesterday."

"Don't worry about it. I just need you to sit there and look your usual professorial self. Lend credibility."

"I feel so cheap."

"I'll buy you a beer afterwards."

"In that case, I'll throw in a couple of pensive looks and a long thought-filled chin rub to really sell it."

Less than a minute later a man walked in. He was about thirty, a little taller than me, and looked to be in good shape. Unlike Edgar, he had no visible tattoos. "Are you Rubia?" he asked, approaching the bar. "I'm Alberto Cuellar."

Rubia came around the bar and shook his hand. She introduced me to him and the three of us sat at my table.

The interview lasted maybe fifteen minutes, Alberto Cuellar deftly answering all of Rubia's questions. His manner made me so comfortable that I even tossed in a question about his experience talking in front of groups because the position required presentations at schools and youth clubs.

He lacked the qualifications of Rubia's previous assistants as well as that of Edgar Ruiz—namely an extensive criminal record. Ironically, that troubled Rubia until he reassured her that he was motivated to help steer kids from drugs and gangs because his two young nephews had recently been gunned down in a gang shootout in LA.

"Guns," I said, shaking my head. "Damn things."

"Professor Pacifist here doesn't believe in guns," Rubia said, rolling her eyes.

The statement didn't seem to have any effect on Cuellar, who simply nodded in acknowledgment.

"What kind of work are you doing now?" Rubia asked.

"I'm a security guard at a grocery store. Not exactly god's calling, if you know what I mean."

Rubia sat quietly for several seconds. "When can you start, Alberto?" she asked, apparently making up her mind on the spot.

He smiled. "Tomorrow. First thing if you need me. And please call me Cuellar. Even my family calls me that."

"Meet me over at the IML office in West Sacramento tomorrow morning at eight and we'll get to work. You can come with me to a presentation I have scheduled later at the middle school."

We shook hands and Cuellar left.

"Do you think he's going to work out?" I asked.

"I have a good feeling about him."

"He's better looking than Edgar, that's for sure."

"I hadn't noticed."

"Yeah, right."

"Don't make me hurt you, professor."

She returned to the bar to finish setting up. I returned to my workers' comp report. A few minutes later I was putting the final touches on my findings about the poor, injured maintenance worker, when my computer announced the arrival of a new e-mail message.

Just a quick look at the "from" line kick-started my heart. Pam1111 sent me another message. I clicked open the e-mail. *You will pay for what you did* was all it said. Embedded below the words, a video or animated graphic repeated a five-second sequence of a woman's face smiling at a camera. The image was blurry, possibly captured by a computer camera. I saved the thumbnail image to my desktop, then opened it with a graphics program. From there I was able to increase the size significantly. That degraded the quality of the image, rendering it even blurrier. Even so, if asked to testify in a court of law, I'd have sworn the woman on the screen was my wife. Her hairstyle and color were Pam's, the facial features, misted in that dreamy blur, couldn't have been anyone else.

"Oh, my god." The room started spinning and I gripped the edge of the table to brace myself.

"What's up, professor?" Rubia, genuinely worried, moved around the bar and approached my table.

Yesterday, when I received the first missive from the alleged Pam, I'd dismissed it as a cruel prank. It became an elaborately cruel prank when Detective Thurber received a phone call from a supposed witness. Now my thoughts and emotions began to seriously consider the reality that she might still be alive. That notion thrilled me, the idea of my wife returning to me after all these years beyond my wildest hopes or prayers. Diminishing this reverie, however, was the obvious—if Pam did indeed live, she hated my guts, thinking I had tried to kill her. Could I get her back and convince her I had nothing to do with that awful car accident?

Rubia turned a chair around and sat opposite me, her arms resting on the seat's back. "Geez, Ray, you look scared out of your mind."

"That's not far off."

"Thirty seconds ago you were your usual boring, middle-aged, professor self. What happened?"

I turned the laptop around so that so she could see the animated image of Pam as I started to describe for her everything that had happened since receiving yesterday's e-mail.

"Wait a minute," she said after I finished my narrative. "How can your wife be alive? Didn't you, or somebody, identify her body?"

"The body had been crushed and burned beyond recognition. They couldn't even use dental records to make a positive identification. Everything pointed to it being Pam—her car, her disappearance. I mean it had to be her, right?"

"Are you sure this video is Pam?"

"Even though it's blurry I think it is. I guess they could have found something online with Pam's image."

"There's no privacy on the Internet."

"She didn't have Facebook or anything like that back then. But who knows where something might have turned up?"

Rubia thought about that for a moment. "So let's just say it is Pam. Why would she suspect you of trying to kill her?"

I shrugged and exhaled. "We did have a fight that morning. A big one."

"All couples fight."

"We hardly ever did. Almost never. And never one like that morning." I turned the computer around back towards me, took another look at the image of Pam, then folded the laptop shut. "I had returned from taking Sara to school that morning. Pam was heading out the door towards work. I said something about Sara's soccer game that weekend and Pam said that she would be going."

"Pretty boring stuff, if you ask me."

"Completely. All I said was 'that would be great' or 'good deal' or something along those lines. Pam went ballistic. She said I was accusing her of being a horrible mother because she had to work so much. See, about that time her company was preparing to do an IPO, you know to go public for the first time by selling stock. Pam was the financial manager of the company and had to work crazy hours for several months. We didn't see her much and she missed a lot of Sara's games and other activities. It did bother me, but I understood and knew it would be over soon."

"That's it? That's the fight?"

"No. In hindsight I should have walked away. But I tried to defuse the situation. Said I didn't mean anything by the comment. She went off at me then. She wouldn't have to work so hard if I made more money. That I lived in an ivory tower and didn't understand how the real world worked. She never talked to me like that before. I knew her dad thought those things about me. But Pam always defended me to him. Anyway, the comment did piss me off and I accused her of having her priorities messed up, that family came first and so on. We went back and forth like that, yelling at each other, for five or ten minutes before she stormed out. I'm pretty sure it was just all the stress she was under at work that made her snap. It was the worst fight of our marriage."

"And she drove off and got in a car accident after that. Maybe that's why she blames you. Because you made her so mad she didn't drive safely."

I shook my head. "The accident didn't happen until that evening. She'd spent a whole day at work. Plenty of time to calm down. God knows why she was driving her car down around Clarksburg. Maybe because she didn't want to come home and face me. I don't know. I called her cell phone several times. I wanted to talk things out. She never picked up."

An older man and a woman came in, regulars, always a vodka martini and a glass of Chardonnay. We were stop one on their daily crawl up Broadway towards Jamie's, where they'd settle in for lunch and more cocktails. I hoped for a more active hobby in my retirement. Then again, who was I to judge?

Rubia pushed the chair away and stood to go serve them. "What are you going to do, Ray?"

I thought for several seconds, my mind grasping for anything that would give it traction.

"I'll take that beer." I'd drink that then go talk to the only guy who'd always maintained Pam never died in that crash.

five

Old Town Auburn, the heart of the Gold Rush community of fifteen thousand people, could have served as the model for Main Street USA. The shops and restaurants, fronted by weathered boardwalks, welcomed passersby with free food samples, water bowls for their dogs, and a simple smile and a wave. Two blocks away Auburn's residents dwelled in quaint homes built in the late 1800s and early 1900s. On a chilly November afternoon, lazy genies of smoke drifted from their chimneys. Quintessential Norman Rockwell.

At the entrance to town I did not venture into this Elysium, instead turning north onto Highway 49, the bedraggled thoroughfare with strip malls, used car dealers, and enough traffic lights to turn a two-mile drive into a twenty-minute odyssey. About half-way through this gauntlet I made a left turn past a Toyota dealership, wound through a housing development, continued down a country road a short ways and then entered the tiny cemetery. For the second time in two days I came to visit my wife.

Pam's headstone was a simple granite affair, no more than two feet tall, etched with her full name, Pamela Reilly Courage, the year she was born, and the year she died. Thirty-nine years in all. I remember the year we both turned thirty-nine. We joked about how old we were getting, that our lives had rounded third base and were heading for home. Get out the rocking chairs and find a glass of water for our dentures. Thirty-nine. Pam never made it past that age. Now at age fifty-two, thirty-nine seemed pretty damned young to me. But I

28

wouldn't want to go back to being thirty-nine again, not if it meant reliving the past thirteen years over again. Sure, there was the good stuff, almost all of it related to raising Sara, the most wonderful daughter a father could ever dream of having. I wouldn't trade that for anything. The constant heartache of Pam's absence, that's the part I wouldn't want to go through again. Rubia was right. I should get over it. Someday. Whenever that would be. Though, in my heart I knew that it would never happen.

I stood next to her grave and spoke to her, wanting to make some connection, to feel her presence, for our souls to embrace, hers now in the afterlife, mine someday to join her forever in a blissful beyond. Just as it never happened before, it did not happen on this day. Irrationally, I concluded that maybe this was a sign that Pam was not really dead, that we had never made a soulful connection because she didn't dwell in an afterlife but somewhere still on earth. Backing away from her grave, I blew her a kiss and returned to my car.

I dreaded the trip's next stop—the reason I'd driven thirty miles into the foothills east of Sacramento. At the ridiculously elaborate guard shack at the entrance to Lake of the Pines, one of the private security officers compared my driver's license photo to the face staring up at him from the car. I mugged a smile.

"Much better looking in the flesh, wouldn't you agree?"

He did not smile. "Are the Reillys expecting you?"

"I doubt it."

"I'm going to have to call them before I can clear your entry." Entering Lake of the Pines sounded like a matter of national security.

"Roger that," I said.

He gave me a dirty look as he grabbed a thin telephone book.

"Their phone number is area code five-three-zero—"

He put up a finger to cut me off, as if I was trying to deceive him with a fake phone number, likely that of my accomplice on the inside who lay in wait to join me with our evil plan to terrorize the good people of Lake of the Pines. He found the number and began dialing.

"Five-three-zero, five-five-five, eighteen-forty-seven," I said, reciting the phone number I still knew by heart. I made him lose track of the number he'd gotten from the book so he had to start all over. The look he gave me would have withered a lesser human.

Five minutes later I sat inside the house where Pam had grown up. Tom and I sat at opposite ends of the couch, Teresa in a plush chair to my right. A Ouija board sat on the coffee table in front of us. Tom and Teresa Reilly were not happy to see me, especially Tom.

"This is a surprise, Ray. I thought you hated it out here." The old man, pushing eighty, was just as feisty as when he used to browbeat the employees at his auto body shop. His paunch had expanded a bit, and his gray hair had thinned since I'd seen him many years ago. His personality appeared not to have changed one bit.

"I never said I hated it. I just prefer the city is all."

"Pam said she used to have to drag you to come out here, even at Thanksgiving and Christmas. A husband should try to respect his wife's wishes when it comes to her family, you know."

God, did I want to argue with him. In the end, that would lead nowhere so I conceded the point. "Guilty as charged, Tom."

An awkward silence ensued. I turned to Teresa and asked how she was doing.

"All right, Ray," she said, her words so slurred it sounded more like *Our rye rye*. Her eyes were bloodshot, her normally pale face a glowing red. She'd once been pretty, the wedding and family photos adorning the walls of their modest home attested to that. After Pam died, she started hitting the bottle hard and I suspected that today wasn't the first in which she was blotto before three in the afternoon.

"Are you going to tell us why you came after all these years, or just sit here and make small talk?"

"Tom," I said. The conversation would not be easy but it was one I needed to have. "I know that you've always believed that Pam didn't die in the accident. That she faked her own death to be free from me."

Tom nodded. "I know it must hurt hearing that, but it's the truth. And you know me, Ray, I don't pull my punches. Straight up, one hundred percent. That's what you get from me."

"And I can appreciate that. In its own heartless way it makes sense." As a former communications professor I did not subscribe to the notion that brutal honesty always fostered positive human relations. "Can I ask you why you embraced the theory that Pam faked her death?"

"Just a father's instinct."

"Did she say she was unhappy with me?"

"Not in so many words. I could tell, though."

"How so?"

"I could just tell."

"Okay, whatever." Despite my self-coaching during the drive out here from Sacramento, I was letting Tom annoy me. I believed his irrational belief in Pam's survival stemmed from denial and nothing more. "The private investigators you've hired, have they found anything?"

"No. Worthless pieces of shit. In this day and age how hard can it be to track down a living, breathing human being? Credit cards, cell phones, surveillance cameras—it's just about impossible to go completely off the grid."

"How many investigators have you hired over the years?"

"Five, counting the one this year. He said Pam left no trail to suggest she survived after the accident. I think that's bullshit."

"It's all bullshit, Tom. Pam's dead," Teresa said. *Sall buh sit ta, puhms ded.*

Tom dismissed his wife with a dirty look.

"And the psychics? Have they shed any light on things?"

"Maybe. They've confirmed that Pam's not on the other side. That she's still alive. One said she was in San Antonio. Another said she was in Cleveland. I hired investigators in both cities but nothing's turned up so far."

I discounted the psychics out of principle. No doubt these con artists could sense the frantic hopes of a father who'd lost his only daughter, telling him whatever it took to perpetuate his beliefs that his loved one still lived and, with that belief, continue to pay for "psychic insight."

"Tell me, Ray. After all these years of you thinking me a crackpot for believing that Pam wasn't killed, why all of a sudden do you give a rat's ass about what I've learned?"

I expected the question. While I didn't love, or even like, my in-laws—grudging acceptance of them the best I could muster—I wanted to avoid hurting them at all costs. Telling Tom that I'd received a message from someone claiming to be Pam could validate his long-held belief about his daughter, giving him false hope. But I owed them the truth.

"I received an e-mail yesterday," I began and proceeded to tell them everything sent to me from the person who was or was not Pam. I spent a good five minutes explaining the argument Pam and I had the morning before she died, leaving nothing out. They needed to know everything, good and bad.

Tom didn't appear to be moved one way or the other. Teresa didn't seem to absorb a word I said, rising from her chair halfway through my narrative to make another gin and tonic.

"Why didn't you tell me about your argument with her before?" he asked.

"I wasn't trying to hide anything. Just didn't think it was relevant. To me Pam was dead. Nothing else really mattered."

"Fits right in with my theory."

"Let's go back again to before the accident," I said. "Are you sure Pam never said anything, or gave you any indication that she was planning to leave me? Or that she hated or disliked me?"

"Like I said, it was a father's instinct. But no, she never said anything like that."

He confirmed what had been nagging at me. The enmity in the e-mails seemed disproportionate to anything I could have possibly done to deserve it. Sure we had the fight that morning, an aberration in our marriage, nothing that rocked its foundation, a nasty dustup awaiting a kiss and make up. Other than that I couldn't think of what I could have done to cause enough pain and bitterness to drive my wife to fake her own death and to return thirteen years later to punish me. I never cheated on, lied to, or abused her. No skeletons hung in my closet. I made every effort to be a good father and a good husband.

If Pam lived, I needed the answer to the question of why she ran. And then I'd need to convince her that she had made a mistake. If Pam did indeed die, then it raised two different questions. Who in the hell chose to impersonate my wife? And why?

The pivot point on which path to pursue was clear—was Pam still alive?

six

Chuck Rattner drove alone, steering his twelve-year-old Hyundai Accent with his knees as he traveled west out of Dayton, Nevada on Highway 50 to his home in the desert. He munched on a double bacon cheeseburger, pausing occasionally to stuff a handful of french fries into his mouth, chasing them down with a swallow of his chocolate milkshake. He used the frayed sleeve of his jacket to wipe his lips before launching another assault on the burger. He finished his lunch, stuffed the wrappers and cup back into the fast food bag, and tossed it out the window.

He took the next exit off the highway and continued several miles before turning onto an unpaved road that led to his house. The day had already been great. Before heading into town he'd received three e-mails from buyers agreeing to meet his sales terms. Then in town he received two e-mails on his cell phone indicating PayPal payments to the tune of $2100 had been sent to him. Life was looking up. He pulled to the side of the dirt road, got out of the car, and opened his battered mailbox. Mostly the same old junk. Then a letter with a $500 check inside from yet another customer. Best day ever!

The house wasn't much, a two bedroom modular, which if he was going to be honest with himself was actually a trailer. The roof leaked in the winter, though the piece of corrugated sheet metal he'd secured on the roof with a dozen bricks seemed to be working for now.

"Fucking cat," he said as he walked inside to the stench of cat shit. Mainly because Rattner was fond of kicking the thing whenever he saw it, the cat hadn't shown himself in months, living off the food strewn about the place whenever Rattner went on one of his errands. He'd locate the shit later, maybe even make a determined effort to find the culprit, but for now he wanted to get online to see if more good news awaited him.

No new e-mails of importance awaited him when he opened his inbox. He cursed. Ten years he'd been playing for the big score, the one that would take him out of a trailer in the desert and into a penthouse in Reno. Reno, hell. He could move to San Francisco with that payday.

He navigated from his e-mail to his website, rattnerdomains.com, "World's Leading Domain Store." That was bullshit of course, but you didn't get out of Dayton, Nevada, with modesty. In his heart, he knew he dwelled in the bush leagues among the domain speculators of the world. Since falling into this career more than ten years ago, he'd managed to amass several thousand web domains. At first he just used his own imagination to think of URLs that individuals or businesses might want.

The porn site names were the easiest to come up with since that was an interest right up his alley. Most of the good names had already been taken by the porn purveyors, though he managed to snag a few that he sold for several thousand each over the years. Then he searched the websites of Fortune 500 companies, movie studios, and pro sports teams to see if any of them had a new product, movie or promotion coming up that would lend itself to a site name he could snatch up before they did.

His inventory of names swelled from a couple of hundred into the thousands when he stumbled onto a shareware program in a dark recess of the Internet. The program searched for and caught URLs the second the current owner's contract for it lapsed. In would swoop "The Ratt Man" to buy it before the owner could do so. He made most of his money selling back these addresses to their original owners. Served the idiots right for being so careless.

He searched to see if his script had netted any new URLs of interest. Nothing decent except for maybe one porn site that he'd consider later. Back on the Available page, his eyes lingered for several seconds on the three prizes in his collection—crazyzebratv.com, crazyzebravideo.com, and crazyzebratube.com. All because he was smart, smarter than that dumbass fighter. The dumbass fighter who now refused to his terms of a million dollars for each one of the domains. That wasn't unreasonable. Hell no, he even offered to throw in for free the .org, .net and .edu version of the domains as well. Stupid motherfucker ... stupid, *rich*, motherfucker refused to pay it. For ten years now he'd offered Yuri "Crazy Zebra" Mastrov the domains and for ten years he'd refused.

Tomorrow his contract for them would lapse. Of course, he would renew them before they expired. That's the way he always did it on all the domains he owned. Buy them for a year, e-mail an offer to likely customers, and if they didn't buy, renew them 364 days later. The first few times he offered the domains to Yuri, the thug had dispatched his lawyers, who threatened to sue him. He called their bluff and the bastards slithered off, his ownership of the domain names bulletproof. This year he thought it might be the year The Crazy Zebra caved.

The sound of a car door closing jolted his attention from the computer screen. Peering out his smeared kitchen window, he saw two men getting out of a white Dodge Challenger.

"What the fuck?" No one ever came out here, which was the way he liked it. These guys looked okay. Bitchin' ride. Would love to have a Challenger. Old school muscle car. Nice.

Rattner opened the door before they could knock.

"Mr. Rattner?" said the taller man. He offered a polite smile. He had light brown skin and dark hair, good-looking like that actor guy whose name Rattner couldn't think of at the moment. The other guy was blond, shorter, solidly built, maybe two hundred and fifty pounds' worth. Both wore suits with open collar dress shirts.

"What do you want?" Rattner said.

"My name is Lobo Hernandez and this is David Bennington," the tall guy said, gesturing towards his companion. John Stamos. That's who he looked like, maybe a little darker skin but definitely John Stamos. "We're here on business. Okay if we go inside?"

Rattner hesitated. The place was a mess and smelled like cat shit. Besides, he did all his business online and no one was supposed to know where he actually lived. "What kind of business?"

"We're here to buy a couple of your websites."

"I do all my sales online."

"Our employer prefers to conduct his business in a face-to-face manner. Either directly, or as in this case, with his trusted employees conducting it for him."

"Who's your employer?"

"Yuri Mastrov."

Rattner felt a big smile cross his face. "Come in, gentlemen," he said, opening the door wider and stepping back to let them in. "I've been hoping to hear from you." Could this day get any better or what?

They settled in at the small kitchen table once Rattner had cleared off several food-caked dishes and a loose stack of papers. "Can I get you guys some coffee or water or something?"

"No thank you," Stamos said. "We would like to take care of business as soon as possible, right Mr. Bennington?"

"Absolutely," Bennington, the stocky blond guy, said. "Let's not waste any time."

"Good," Rattner said. "Will you be writing a check or using a credit card? If it's a check it will have to be a certified or cashier's check. Not that I don't believe Mr. Mastrov is good for it, but it's company policy."

"Company policy," Stamos said, smiling. "I like that. There's no need to worry, however. We plan to pay cash."

"Cash! All the better. Is it out in your car or something?"

"We have it, don't worry. Before we complete the transaction I want to be sure we are clear. You are selling crazyzebratv.com, crazyzebravideo.com and crazyzebratube.com, correct?"

"Correct. And I'm even throwing in dot org, dot net and dot edu."

"Very generous of you," Bennington said.

"So if we pay you today, you will transfer ownership to Crazy Zebra Empire immediately, is that right?" Stamos continued.

"Sure, I'll do it while you're here if you want."

"Fair enough. Now, what if you did not renew your contract on the sites, which I believe expire tomorrow?"

"Then they would be back in the public domain for anyone to buy,

but that ain't going to happen." Rattner's hackles rose. Now he got it—
these guys wanted to negotiate the price.

"No need to get upset Mr. Rattner. I just wanted to understand. I
don't know a lot about how these things work, so I wanted to be sure."

"No problem." Rattner felt a little calmer. The man had an easy
manner that Rattner trusted.

"All right then, let's get this done," Stamos said, retrieving his
wallet from his back pocket. He pulled out a dollar bill and placed it on
the table.

"What the fuck's that?" Rattner said.

"Our payment for the websites."

"What? What are you trying to pull? It's three million, not a cent
less. What the fuck?"

"You need to reconsider your price," Bennington said. "I think
you'll agree that a dollar is a fucking bargain." From behind his back
he pulled out a huge gun.

"Hey, I don't want any trouble, okay?"

"Neither do we," Stamos said.

"Can't we come to some reasonable compromise?" The gun
scared him, it did. But he'd been dreaming about that three million
dollars for ten years. Ten years. It was his big payout. He couldn't just
wet his pants and cave because they bluffed him with a gun. "How
about half a million for each site? That's one and a half million. That's
more than fair."

"Mr. Bennington, do you think that's a fair price?" Stamos said,
his eyes locked on Rattner.

"I don't," said Bennington.

Rattner watched in horror as the man named Bennington pulled
the trigger and shot him.

seven

Demetrio Gutierrez lived in a house on Sacramento's Northgate Boulevard, for which the label "modest" would be a huge exaggeration, consisting of two bedrooms, a single bathroom, a tiny kitchen, and a cramped space that served as living room, dining area, study, and sleeping area for the occasional guest.

His parents, Carlos and Juanita, settled in the house fourteen years earlier after emigrating from Mexico City to find better lives for themselves and their two children. Theirs was the only residential structure on a street comprised mainly of shuttered or struggling businesses. The next-door neighbors consisted of a smog-testing shop and a self-service car wash, while across the busy four-lane street were a medical marijuana dispensary and a Food 4 Less, whose parking lot served as a haven for drug dealers catering to customers seeking to supplement their purchases at the marijuana store with other pharmaceuticals.

Eighteen-year-old Demetrio and his sixteen-year-old sister Lucinda had long ago been warned by their parents to avoid the grocery store and the dispensary, warnings both heeded. When school ended each day, brother and sister took a city bus to downtown Sacramento, where they transferred to another bus that took them to within two blocks of their Del Paso Heights neighborhood home.

The journey took an hour and fifteen minutes each school day, which meant they arrived home at four-fifteen in the afternoon. I was waiting on their front porch when they opened the chain-link gate at the front of their yard and headed towards me.

"Mr. Ray, how are you?" Demetrio said to me enthusiastically, as if he hadn't seen me in years. He shook my hand vigorously. He was a small boy with wiry limbs who wore his dark hair short.

"Lucinda, how did your Algebra test go today?" I asked.

"Pretty well, I think. It was easier than I expected." Lucinda was pretty and as smart as her older brother. The two-block walk from the bus stop to home often came with catcalls and worse from young male drivers and street punks, offenses that she'd long ago learned to ignore with stoic resolve, even as her protective brother gave each culprit a long, dirty look.

We entered the house, Lucinda heading directly to the bedroom she and her brother shared to start her homework. Demetrio offered me some orange juice and something to eat, which I declined. He proceeded to pour himself some juice and prepare a small plate of crackers. He joined me at the kitchen table, retrieved his laptop from his backpack, and turned it on.

"How is Rubia doing?" he said.

"She's doing great. She told me to give you her best." Rubia had introduced me to Demetrio and his family six years ago, back when he was just starting middle school. She had recently opened IML, when one day a middle-aged Mexican man walked in and introduced himself as Carlos Gutierrez. They spoke for twenty minutes during which time Carlos told her about his children, how gifted they were in school, and how he worried about them growing up in such a rough neighborhood. He had a one-man gardening business, while his wife worked as a maid at a Motel 6, their combined earnings insufficient to afford better accommodations. Upon meeting the children, Rubia knew that Carlos's characterization of them as gifted went beyond parental boasting. She took them under her wing to help keep them from succumbing to the street, and brought me in to help them achieve their full academic potential.

Demetrio's laptop came to life and he navigated to the web page we'd both come to know quite well.

"School still going well?" I said, before we started in.

"Yeah," he said, with less than his usual enthusiasm.

"What's wrong?"

"Nothing."

Demetrio and Lucinda attended The Buckingham School, the most exclusive high school in Sacramento. Tuition ran thirty-thousand dollars a year. After reading the dismal performance statistics for the local public school when Demetrio was about to enter ninth grade, I helped the Gutierrez family complete the scholarship and admission application to Buckingham. He was awarded a full scholarship based on his academics and the parents' modest earnings. Two years later Lucinda received the same award.

"I can tell something is bothering you," I said.

"I don't know. It's just this whole college thing is intimidating me. That's all everybody in my class is talking about. Which Ivy League schools they're going to apply to. Who they know at Stanford who will get them in. I don't know if I can measure up to all that."

I smiled and shook my head. "What's your grade point average?"

"You already know that." He didn't like to talk about himself, especially about anything that might sound like bragging.

"Right, four-point-five weighted, four-point-oh unweighted. All A's in the toughest courses at your school."

He blushed as I continued on.

"What did you get on the SAT?"

"I don't remember."

"Yeah, right. But just in case, I'll remind you that it was 2310 out of 2400. I bet no one at Buckingham did better."

"Yeah, one girl I know did."

"Really?" I was surprised, not too many students scored above 2300 on the SAT.

"Yeah, Elena Mastrov scored a perfect 2400."

"That's impressive. Do you have a lot of classes with her?" I was curious if the girl had the practical smarts that Demetrio did or if she was simply a test-taking savant.

"We're in almost all of the same classes. It's a small school. I heard another girl also got a perfect score but I don't know her very well."

"Well, I wouldn't feel compelled to take the SAT again just to try for a perfect score," I said, giving him a light punch to the shoulder.

"Don't worry about that," he said smiling. "Once was enough for me. Elena took it four times, no wonder she jumped up from 1750 to 2400. The last time was in June when I took it at McClatchy. She must have been in a different room than me because I never saw her, even though G's through M's were supposed to be in the same room."

"Let's get started," I said, pulling my chair over so that we could both see the laptop's screen, which was displaying The Common Application website. The previous week we had completed most of the required information. Today, the goal was to review it for typos and omissions.

"Are you still sure about applying early decision to Occidental?" I said. "It's binding. You won't be able to go to any of your other schools." I knew that Oxy was his top choice, though I also knew he had very good chances of getting into the other schools where he planned to apply—Stanford, UC Berkeley, UCLA, Cal Poly and San Diego State.

"I'm positive."

I had accompanied Demetrio and his mom on visits to all his colleges. While he liked every one of the schools on his list, Occidental had impressed him the most. He liked the small college feel, and it offered a biology major and a minor in neuroscience, the research area he hoped to pursue. One of the neuroscience professors at the school talked with him for an hour on their shared interest on photo-transduction proteins, whatever the hell that was. Sealing the deal for him was our meeting with the financial aid office which, after reviewing the family's finances and Demetrio's academic record, all but promised a full-ride financial package.

For the next ten minutes I read his application essay and offered him a few minor suggestions. Next I reviewed the supplemental questions specifically for his Occidental application. It all looked great.

"All right," I said to him an hour after my arrival. "I'll be back on the nineteenth and we'll finalize this. The early decision deadline is the twentieth, so once we finish reviewing it you should be able to hit 'send.'"

eight

"You're late." Yuri Mastrov spoke without lifting his eyes from the computer screen in front of him. Crazy Zebra Empires' stock shares were up five points on the NASDAQ, continuing a recent good run.

"We had to do a little clean up that took longer than I expected," Lobo said. The chief of security for Crazy Zebra Empires drew up a chair across from his boss's desk.

"Things worked out according to plan, I assume," Mastrov said.

"As of tomorrow morning all three sites will be public domain. You can buy them for less than ten bucks apiece."

At forty-three years-old, Mastrov could probably still compete in Mixed Martial Arts, the sport he dominated as a world champion from his late teens to late twenties. Standing six-four and weighing two hundred fifty pounds, with a huge head that each morning he shaved meticulously except for his perfectly manicured Van Dyke beard, he didn't just command a room when he entered; he intimidated it. *Fortune* ranked him as one of the fifty richest men in the world, a stature earned from hard work and an obsession for detail. He picked up the phone from his desk and called his director of technology.

"They'll be available one second after midnight tonight. I expect them to be mine by one minute past the hour. Are we clear?" Not claiming the Crazy Zebra URLs had been a rare oversight for Mastrov, an inattention to detail for which he ultimately blamed himself, though he had fired his entire IT staff ten years ago when he learned that someone else had beat him to the coveted web addresses.

Mastrov set down the phone and turned his attention to Lobo. It had been so long ago when he first saw the then seventeen-year-old Puerto Rican, an aspiring MMA light-heavyweight who exhibited the ruthlessness of a sociopath in the ring, but lacked the talent to make it to even the sport's mid-rankings. Mastrov knew the man's ruthlessness could prove beneficial to his emerging business interests. For his part, Lobo became a fighter as a means to leave the slums of Miami and not necessarily to pursue a dream of becoming world champion. When Mastrov had offered the teenager a job with Crazy Zebra Empires for three times what he earned as a fighter, Lobo jumped at the chance. Fifteen years later, he had risen from odd jobs to head of security for a multibillion-dollar corporation.

"How are the other matters shaping up?"Mastrov asked.

"Perfectly. We've set surveillance recorders in the homes of all of the CEOs you asked for. We finished tapping into their computers yesterday. Their corporate offices are proving a bit more problematic because several of them have sweeps done on a regular basis, but our guy is working on that. We have an idea for using radio waves that should work out fine. That NSA guy you hired is worth every nickel you're paying him. He knows all the tricks."

Mastrov smiled at the compliment. He'd lured a mid-level NSA spook away from his federal job with its cushy pension by offering him five times his salary and buying him a mansion in Granite Bay. The investment had already paid off, today's stock price a testimony to that fact.

"The other surveillance is going well, too," Lobo continued. "I seriously doubt there's anything to it. But it's got my full attention. You can count on that, boss."

"Good. So without getting into any of the details, can you tell me why the business in Nevada took longer than expected?"

"Root."

"What about him?" Mastrov had hired Daniel Bennington a few years back after he had been expelled from the UFC circuit for multiple infractions, including beating up one of his opponents in an alley two days before their match. His nickname, Root, was short for "Root of all Evil," his fighting handle and a spot-on description of his character. Mastrov saw the same things in Root as he did in Lobo, adding him to his collection of thugs who exhibited loyalty and enthusiastic violence on command. Unlike Lobo, Root had grown up rich and spoiled. Beating the crap out of his schoolmates on a weekly basis proved his favorite activity. His dad helped channel that energy by introducing him to martial arts and boxing, launching him into a mediocre UFC career before his expulsion from the sport.

"He doesn't follow orders very well and, as usual, was reckless."

"You need to mentor him." The two men's personalities were too much alike, Mastrov mused. No wonder they didn't always see eye to eye.

"I'll keep trying."

"Do that. And keep me posted on your surveillance. I don't want anything getting past us."

Once Lobo left the office, Mastrov stood and opened the side door that led to his private gym. He changed from his ten thousand dollar custom-made suit into his workout clothes—a T-shirt, baggy shorts, and running shoes. The simple attire returned him to his origins, made him remember his own impoverished life, the son of Russian immigrants with nothing, not even love for one another.

He loaded three hundred pounds on the barbell and began bench pressing the weight, firing off five repetitions in short order. Ten. Fifteen. Twenty. Barely winded, he reset the bar on the rack and sat upright to rest his muscles. He thought about the journey of his life.

When he was thirteen years old, his mom bought him a black and white striped sweater. He wore it the first day of middle school. At lunch one of the older kids, an eighth grader, made fun of the sweater, calling Mastrov a zebra. Mastrov never felt such embarrassment or anger before. He used his fury to pummel the poor kid, and three of his friends, before four teachers finally restrained him. He served a three-day suspension from school. Beating up those boys had exhilarated him like nothing before and he knew he'd found his life's calling. He used every free moment working out and practicing martial arts, vowing to become a world champion fighter. He wore the zebra sweater every day the rest of the school year, even when the temperatures pushed a hundred degrees, daring anyone to make fun of it. Behind his back, kids started calling him the "Crazy Zebra." Mastrov heard them. Rather than anger him, it amused him and he knew what his nickname would be when he started his career in Mixed Martial Arts.

When his attention turned more to business than fighting, he founded Crazy Zebra Empires, which began as a single gym devoted to training mixed martial arts fighters. Three years later he owned a hundred gyms focused less on fighters and more on the general population. A few years after that, Crazy Zebra Empires became publicly owned. With the infusion of cash from the initial public offering, Mastrov created the Crazy Zebra Television Network, which broadcasted mixed martial art matches, news, and features around the clock.

Skeptics had scoffed at the idea of a television network with such a narrow focus and a relatively small market. That was several billion dollars in earnings ago. With the new web addresses he'd obtain just after midnight, he'd be able to expand his network's reach by capitalizing on the power of the Internet. Sure, he had a couple of websites already, but he wanted to own all the addresses that related to the Crazy Zebra brand. Maybe not a big deal in the grand scheme of his business, but not having those addresses had nagged at him, a two-bit punk trying to extort him for what was rightfully his. No more.

Mastrov indulged himself a rare smile before settling onto his back and starting his second set of bench presses.

November 13

nine

"If you're not here for business, I don't have time for your questions," said the overweight man of about sixty with a jowly, florid face. It was the morning after my visit with Pam's parents.

I had known Larry Slager for thirty seconds and already disliked him. He spit a stream of chewing tobacco in the dirt between us. Slager's Towing Company didn't reside in Locke proper, occupying a couple of acres more inland, almost equidistant between the river and Interstate 5. A small structure about the size of a suburban garage sat directly in front of me, his office I guessed. What looked to be a small house lay several hundred feet beyond the office. In between the two I could see three large tow trucks designed to carry oversized payloads on their flatbeds. One truck was outfitted with a large plate of thick steel across the grill.

"Why does that rig have a sheet of metal across the front?" I said pointing at the truck in question.

"Sometimes you got to push shit out the way to get to the shit you came to haul. Ain't gonna fuck up my truck and it's faster than using a fucking winch, so I built that piece of shit over there."

"Creative." I was referring to his ability to use the noun "shit" for pretty much anything. The affirming nod he gave to my assessment suggested he thought I meant the sheet-metal enhanced truck.

Slager spit again. "Look buddy, I really do need to get to work."

"This won't take long. I promise. And it's very important to me."

"Twenty bucks."

46

"Excuse me."

"It'll cost you twenty bucks. Every minute I waste talking to you, I'm losing money."

I doubted that Larry Slager earned anything approaching two dollars a minute. Nevertheless, I pulled a twenty out of my wallet and handed it over to him. Paying someone for an interview went against my principles. Sometimes you have to make an exception. Somewhere in Asia, the Dalai Lama no doubt felt a stab of heartburn over the negative Karma I had set in motion.

"Now, what do you want to know?"

"It's been awhile, thirteen years to be exact. There was an accident on the River Road near Clarksburg. There was a fatality."

"Thirteen years ago, are you shitting me? I bet two or three people a year die on the River Road. Drink too much then drive into the river and drown. Stupid fucks."

I had to be careful here. I'd come to determine if Slager had been the one to hit my wife with one of his big tow trucks, information he would not want to offer up. An approach too direct might spook him and he'd dismiss me in a heartbeat.

"How long have you lived here?" I asked, feeling a need to take on the subject of the accident a bit more subtly, though I had no clue about how to do so. Getting him to keep talking appeared to be the best strategy I could summon in the moment.

"My whole life. Four generations of Slagers have been raised here. Now it's just me and my brother."

I detected some bitterness in his voice at the mention of his brother. "Your brother in the towing business, too?"

Another spit. "Nope. Daddy left him one hundred percent of the family farming business, not to mention the house we both grew up in. Baby brother went to college, see. As if that counts for shit. Fresno State. Earned himself a fancy degree. I guess I weren't good enough to plant tomatoes and corn. Now he plays golf three days a week, sends his kids to private schools, and doesn't say hi, bye, or shit in your eye to me."

Hit a bit of a nerve there. A change of subject was in order. "Well, clearly you've got one heckuva a great business going here."

"Fuckin' A."

"How long have you been in business?"

"Going on twenty-eight years. Didn't have everything handed to me like he did. Built this from the ground up. One truck, then two, then three, then four."

I looked about the yard again and saw only the three trucks. "Four?"

He saw me looking at the inventory on his property and understood immediately. "Got one out on assignment right now. See, I make most of my money renting out my trucks to freelancers. I drive one truck for the calls that come in here, but I can handle that with one truck and just me. The other trucks are for renting out to drivers who can do the work but can't afford the overhead of owning their own rigs."

"Interesting. How long ago did you buy your second truck?"

"Hell, I don't remember, something like eight, nine years ago or so."

"So you were a one truck shop before that."

"Nothing gets past you, does it? You looking to get into the towing business or something? 'Cause if you are I ain't telling you shit. Don't need no more competition."

"No, nothing like that. Just curious is all." The fact he only had one truck thirteen years ago probably ruled out the possibility he'd rented out the truck that may have killed Pam. "I just heard that you ran this great towing business and it got me thinking back to when a friend of mine got killed in an accident on River Road."

"I already told you I can't remember every car that drives into the river."

"This one was a little different," I said. "Didn't plunge into the river. This was an accident where the car hit something then burst into flames. I was wondering if maybe you got called in to remove the wreckage."

"Why do you give a shit if I did?"

"It was someone I knew. I kind of wanted to know what happened is all. The police report didn't reveal much. I figured a professional like you, who hauls away all kinds of wrecks, might have some insight

48

based on your experience."

"I don't haul away wrecks, at least not cars. But come to think of it, I do remember that accident. Fucking cops even came to talk to me about it. Some asshole told them that maybe it was me ran into that car then drove away. They figured that whatever hit that car had to be a big mofo like my truck."

"What did you tell them?"

"After I told them to go fuck themselves, I told them where I was when the accident happened. Drinking beer in West Sac, at the Sail Inn, like I did most nights back then. Never heard nothing more from the cops after that. Figured they checked in with the bartender and four or five other people who saw me there."

Without access to the police report on the accident I didn't realize that they'd already talked to Slager and cleared him as a hit-and-run suspect. It would have saved me the trip, twenty bucks, and the pleasure of Larry Slager's company. Maybe Detective Lewis wasn't as lazy as Carla Thurber thought.

"I told that cop that I seen a rig like mine near Freeport, about twenty minutes after they said the accident happened," Slager continued. It was heading north away from the accident. When you're in the business, you notice shit like that."

"Did you recognize what towing company it was or see the driver?"

"Too dark to see the driver, besides I'd had a few beers. And I didn't see a company name or anything on the rig, which I thought was kind of weird. Back then there weren't more than three or four of us in the big rig towing business. And I knew them all. That truck wasn't from 'round here."

"What did the cops say when you told them that?"

"Nothing. I don't think they gave a rat's ass what I said once they figured they couldn't pin it on me."

ten

I sat at the bar inside Iron Grill Restaurant awaiting my order of a turkey sandwich and a green salad.

I took a sip of iced tea and turned my thoughts to the messages and the blurry image that was maybe my wife. So far, I had resisted replying to the messages, believing that to do so would merely encourage the prankster. But I couldn't deny outright that Pam might still be alive. With that possibility came the necessity to contact the sender.

I met Pam Reilly in my junior year at San Jose State. She was sitting in one of four cushy chairs at a coffee table inside the student union. I had seen her around campus before, a cutie with long light-brown hair and a trim, athletic figure. My college dating life the first two years had been uneventful, maybe a dozen first dates and less than a handful of second ones. When one of the students collected her things and vacated the chair next to the girl, I seized the opportunity and plopped into the chair, pulled out a book, and pretended to read. So many years later I've forgotten the actual line I used to start the conversation, though I do remember in that first talk I learned all about the finance major who shared my passion for baseball, dogs, reading, and reruns of *The Twilight Zone*. That first conversation led to lunch that same day, followed by dinner the next night, then a movie, then a relationship followed by a marriage as good as I could have ever envisioned.

Our marriage wasn't perfect, if there is such a thing; rather, we

50

were perfect for one another. I'm not sure which I valued more my love *for* her or my friendship *with* her. Our love and friendship grew stronger and more intertwined with every passing day, each passing year until at some point I became part of her and she part of me. Call it corny and unoriginal. It just happened to be true. When Sara became part of our family she did not divide us or weaken the relationship Pam and I had as happens to many couples. If anything she made it stronger, giving our marriage a mission to provide our daughter the fullest life possible, enabled by the best education, strongest moral compass, and deepest love we could provide.

God, did I miss her. I took out the creased photo of her that I carried in my wallet. In the photograph, taken at one of our neighborhood Fourth of July block parties, she's laughing, her eyes alive with joy, someone at ease with herself. The photo perfectly captured her. In this age of cell phone photos, cloud storage and social media, I knew carrying a photograph was old school, even quaint. I didn't care. I loved that picture and the feeling it brought every time I looked at it.

I reached inside my coat and pulled out my cell phone. Rather than reply to one of the e-mails from Pam1111, I created a new one. I didn't want the accusing and malicious content of those messages to poison my message. I pondered what to put in the address line and what appeal to use in the message. Was I writing to a ghost? My wife? Some psychopath? There weren't appropriate words for all three. I settled for the following:

> *Subject: Who are you?*
> *I have received the e-mails you have sent, including the animated photo. You claim to be my wife, Pam. But the woman I knew and loved for so many years would never say what you wrote in those messages. She would never accuse me of harming her because she would know that is the farthest thing from the truth. Whoever you are, I ask you to respect my memories of my beloved wife and refrain from contacting me again.*
> *--RC*

I re-read the e-mail three times, wondering if I'd set the right tone. Should I have been harsher in an effort to scare the writer away? Or, should I have gone for the long shot of the writer actually being Pam and made a direct appeal to her by avowing my innocence and my love? In the end, I sent the e-mail the way it stood. When I looked to my right, I saw Detective Thurber seated beside me.

"Fan mail from some flounder," I said, pointing at the sent e-mail, embarrassed to not have seen her sooner. I stuffed my cell phone back into my coat pocket.

"Excuse me?"

"Fan mail from some flounder. It's from the *Rocky and Bullwinkle* cartoon show back in the 60s. Rocky finds a message in a bottle and Bullwinkle asks if it's fan mail—"

She put up her hand to cut me off. I doubted Carla Thurber whiled away her idle moments of youth watching cartoons, more likely preferring the wacky antics of Detective Joe Friday on *Dragnet*.

"I hope I'm not interrupting your lunch," she said, not sounding like she really meant it.

"My order will be here soon." Where the hell was my sandwich, anyway?

"This won't take long."

"How did you know to find me here?"

"Luck. I went to the Say Hey because I heard that you used that as an office but it was closed. I was driving back to the station and saw your car parked on the street out front."

Plausible. Only two blocks separated the Say Hey from Iron Grill. Her colleague, Lieutenant Trujillo, knew that I worked at the Say Hey.

"Have you heard anything more from your anonymous informant?" I asked, injecting as much sarcasm into the question as I could summon.

"No. Not yet. I did go over the file again and I am going to reopen the investigation just to be sure everything was done by the book."

"You're not going to say something looks 'hinky'? Or that the file is 'hinky' or any other hinkyism? Or is it only movie cops who use that word?"

"Don't fuck with me, Courage. I came here as a courtesy to let you know that I was reopening the case, at least for a few days."

"Thanks," I said to Thurber. At last, my sandwich and salad arrived. I waited for the waitress to leave before continuing.

"You don't seem very happy that I'm trying to find the person who killed your wife in that accident."

I shrugged. Truth was, after the accident, the shock, then the grief, and finally the enduring sorrow, muffled the rage inside me. Thirteen years later the rage only occasionally flared, and even then it was tempered by time. When it did flare, my anger was extinguished by the sheer logic that the other driver would never be found. Did I want the person to be found? Yes, sure. Would it bring Pam back? No, and any justice heaped on the person who hit my wife's car and left her there to die would fall hopelessly short of alleviating the tragedy of her death, and the pain it brought to those who loved her.

"I guess I should appreciate that you're reopening the case," I said between bites. "I'm just concerned that the ridiculous phone call you got the other day makes you think I had something to do with her death."

"I never said you were a suspect."

"You implied as much."

"Maybe. But as far as I'm concerned, at this moment, your wife died in a hit-and-run *accident.*"

"Okay." I set the sandwich down and started in on the salad.

"Do you have any idea why was she driving down in Clarksburg?"

"None. I've asked myself that a million times. She didn't know anybody down there as far as I know."

"Could she have been driving around to kill time after work because she didn't want to come home?"

I gave Thurber a mockingly sweet smile. "Who in their right mind wouldn't want to come home to somebody as charming as me?"

"You need to take this seriously," she said.

"Believe me, I am." She had no idea how seriously I took this. The messages I'd received rattled me. If they stopped after the e-mail I'd just sent then maybe I could feel better. If they didn't, I would have to find her, be it Pam or someone about whose motives I couldn't even guess. Either way, I wasn't going to tell Thurber about the messages. Or that I had begun my own investigation.

"Who would have known that you and she had a fight the morning of her death?"

"I told you we didn't have a fight."

Not much she could do with that, lacking any evidence to refute my recollection. She stood up and started to leave. "You're not helping yourself here," she said.

My cell phone vibrated loudly in my jacket, announcing the arrival of a new e-mail. It had to be a reply to my recent e-mail. Reflexively, I blushed.

"Fan mail from some flounder?" she said as she stood and left the restaurant.

eleven

I pondered how to respond to the e-mail I received from Pam1111 at the end of lunch. Though part of me believed my request to be left alone might convince the sender to stop, I knew such a belief was little more than wishful thinking. The response did not shed any new light on the sender's identity, but it did offer some encouragement.

Dana Krabbe's physical presence could only be called unfortunate. I don't want to sound judgmental or sexist. My guess would be that Dana would describe herself using that adjective or something similar. Sixty-six years old, she suffered from dandruff, psoriasis, halitosis, diabetes, fibromyalgia and obesity. I'm not a doctor, and have never played one on TV, so these diagnoses were not made by me but communicated by Dana in the first five minutes of our conversation.

"I always liked your wife," she said, picking at a patch of red, flaky skin on her right arm. "She didn't treat me shitty like some of the people at that company did. Respected me."

"She was your direct supervisor?" After receiving the second e-mail, I began racking my brain for names of Pam's former co-workers, especially the people she worked with closely. Pam had three employees who reported to her. I couldn't come up with Ron's or Jason's last names, but for some reason Dana Krabbe's name stuck in my mind. Tracking her down took only a few minutes using Facebook, my cell phone, and GPS.

We sat in her living room, a small space smelling of stale cigarettes and cluttered with gossip magazines and tabloid newspapers.

Two opened packs of Camel Lights sat on the coffee table next to an open box of Cheez-Its and an orange ceramic ashtray overflowing with butts. The carpet needed a good vacuuming and shampooing. A Chihuahua sniffed my leg, skittering away every time I reached down to pet him.

"Yes. The best boss I ever had."

"What was your job?"

"I was an accounting tech. Mainly I just ran spreadsheets, compiled data for reports, that kind of thing."

The dog came back for another sniff. "What's your dog's name?"

"Steven." A large flake of skin tumbled off her arm and landed on the floor. My gag reflex forced me to cover my mouth.

"That's a nice name," I said, trying restore my composure.

"Named him after Steven Tyler of Aerosmith. I think he is *so* handsome."

"Yes, handsome," I said. The image in my head of Steven Tyler, dressed like my grandmother with a mouth that would shame Jagger, did not help my gag reflex issue. "Do you keep in touch with any of your colleagues from work? You know, like Ron or Jason. I think those are their names, the guys who worked in the finance department."

"*Phfft*. Those guys. Jason Upland and Ron begins with a P … ah, I can't remember. Oh, wait, it's Patel. Those guys. They both looked down on me back then. Them with their MBAs and me with a high school diploma. Thought their shit didn't stink. Pam was the only one who treated me nice."

I smiled. Steven Tyler finished sniffing my right leg and moved on to my left.

"I'm so sorry what happened to her," Dana continued. "Such a shame."

I nodded to acknowledge her condolences. "Do you happen to remember anything about Pam's last day at work?"

"Oh, gosh. That was so long ago that I barely remember working there myself. Less than a year after the accident, I left to go work for the state. Needed the pension. Ten years of civil service didn't get me much. When you put it together with my Social Security check it's enough to eek by on."

I waited to see if she might be able to answer my question. A timer dinged in the kitchen.

"That's the coffee. I started a pot when I got your call. Would you like a cup?"

"Sure, that would be nice. Thank you. Black is fine."

She returned and handed me a mug lettered with the message *Resistance is Futile: The Chihuahua must be obeyed.* Steven Tyler stared at me as if to drive home the point, and perhaps for my earlier gagging episode. Dana settled back in her chair.

"Now what were we talking about?" she asked.

"Pam's last day at work. Do you remember anything about it? Was she upset? Did anything happen?"

She took a sip of coffee and thought. "I do remember she came in that morning very upset. That wasn't like her. She was always so up in the morning, always saying good morning to me and everybody else. She was upbeat all the time, usually."

After our argument, she came in to work still upset. That made sense.

"I didn't see her again until later. She was in meetings all morning. Back then she was in meetings all the time. There was a lot going on, what with that IPO thing. And our office, especially Pam, was right in the middle of it. We were in charge of putting together the prospectus and all the public documents for the people who wanted to invest."

The IPO. That had been the source of our friction. Pam had to work night and day seven days a week for months to get the company ready for it's initial public offering. Her bosses were under a lot of pressure to get it done, get it done right, and get it done on time, right after the first of the upcoming year. Her bosses put the pressure on Pam and the strain began to show, culminating in our argument. In the perfect world of hindsight, I should have walked away from the fight that morning.

"Did you see her that afternoon at all?" I brought the coffee mug towards my lips before noticing some debris of dubious appearance floating on top. I set the mug down. Steven glared at me. Really.

"No. Like I said she was in those meetings. Then she went to lunch and I never saw her again."

This visit had been a waste of time. Poor Dana Krabbe would shed no light on Pam's final hours. I stood and thanked her for her time.

"You know, I did see her right before lunch."

I stopped and turned back towards her.

"She just got out of her meeting and she looked like she had been crying. Her eyes were all red and kind of puffy like."

"Had she been crying earlier, when you saw her first thing in the morning?"

Krabbe shook her head. "I don't think so. She seemed more angry than anything. She definitely hadn't been crying. But she was then, right before lunch time."

"Did she say anything to you? Like maybe why she was so upset."

"Not really." She scratched her head, causing a blizzard of dandruff particles to fall and settle on her shoulder. Not exactly a lovely winter scene. I felt really bad for her.

"You have my number and my e-mail address," I said. "If you can think of anything else, please contact me any time. I really appreciate you seeing me on such notice."

"Okey dokey, artichokee." She got up and showed me to the door. Just as I was leaving her house, she said, "I didn't mention that Pam had asked me about our company's EAP program."

"Employee Assistance Program?" I was familiar with the term because they had an EAP program at Sac State. Employees could consult with a psychologist or other mental health professional up to ten times a year for free.

Krabbe nodded. "She knew that I used the program quite a bit. With all my medical conditions and all, it messes with your head. She asked me for the number of the psychologist that I saw so I gave it to her. Sounded to me like she meant to go see him that very same day."

"You wouldn't happen to remember the psychologist's name, would you?"

"That's a tough one. Been a long time since I seen him. You know that EAP thing was supposed to be anonymous. To the company I mean. They're not supposed to know you're seeing a shrink. You know, so they can't hold it against you or fire you or something. After about a year of seeing this guy, the HR department called me in and said I'm abusing the program, and if I wanted to continue seeing the shrink, I'd have to do it through my medical plan. So much for anonymous."

"So you don't remember his name."

"Hold on." She went down the hallway and entered one of the rooms. She returned a couple of minutes later and handed me a business card. "You can keep it. I don't have any reason to see him anymore. He didn't do me a dang lick of good in the first place."

In the living room, Steven Tyler started to lick his tiny testicles. Time for me to go.

In my car, I took yet another look at the e-mail:

> *You say you meant no harm to me. How can I believe you? You set in motion some bad things. I'm not sure how to react to your e-mail.*

That was it, four short sentences. Three things struck me. First, I "set in motion some bad things." Things as in plural. That sounded like several things, not just Pam's death, resulted from our argument that morning. Not sure what that referred to. Second, the author did not leave a name, not Pam's or anyone else's. Did that mean the sender was abandoning the ruse that he or she was Pam? Or was it simply an oversight? Third, the first two sentences told me that I might be able to engage in a dialogue with the sender. If I could do that, I held out hope of meeting him or her face to face.

November 14

twelve

"It's a courtesy more than anything," Carla Thurber said to Tom Reilly as the old man raked leaves in his front yard. "You know, to let you and your wife know, as parents, that we're taking a second look at the circumstances surrounding your daughter's death."

"It's about goddamned time is all I can say. Now maybe someone can find her and help protect her."

"Excuse me?"

"The investigation was a joke. That detective went through the motions. Didn't put any effort into it. If he had he would have discovered that Pam was still alive."

"Detective Lewis had a distinguished career with the department, Mr. Reilly." She felt the need to put up some defense of Lewis, for the integrity of the department if nothing else.

"Bullshit." He attacked a swath of leaves with impressive athleticism. "You wouldn't be here if you didn't think the same thing."

He had her there so she kept quiet. The old guy had to be around eighty and his mind and body seemed that of a much younger man. Though paunchy, his forearm muscles rippled with each stroke of the rake and his blue eyes pierced her each time he glanced her way.

"He wouldn't listen to me back then when I told him that my daughter was still alive. He looked at me as if I was some kind of crazy man. A loon."

"That was in the file," Thurber said. "Your statement is fully documented."

"And no doubt filed away where it never saw the light of day."

"There really is no reason to believe that your daughter is still alive, though we will of course look at every possibility. My main focus is to see if the investigation was thorough, and to determine if we might be able to find out who crashed into your daughter's car and the circumstances leading up to it."

"I still think she's alive. Hell, I know she's alive."

"Let's revisit what you told Detective Lewis, okay?"

"Fine."

"A couple of things in particular interest me. First, you said your daughter wasn't happy in her marriage to Ray. Secondly, you said you wouldn't be surprised if she staged her own death to escape her marriage. That right there is a very strong statement. Do you have anything that would back it up?"

"It's a father's instinct. I never liked Ray. Hoity-toity college professor. You know my daughter spent seven years after graduating from college following his sorry ass around the country so he could get two more college degrees. Took her up to Seattle where he got his PhD in 'communications,' whatever the fuck that is. Pam couldn't really get her career going until they'd settled, finally, in Sacramento, when his highness finally got a full-time job teaching at Sac State. By then they were both about thirty years old. Pam, smart as she was, probably would have been a vice president or something if she'd gone out and got a real job right out of college."

"Did you get a sense that Pam resented all that—putting her career on hold, following her husband up to Seattle?"

"Not in so many words. But like I said, a father can tell these things."

"Did you ever hear your son-in-law threaten your daughter?"

"No. He would never do anything so stupid in front of me. He'd know I would do something about it if he ever did."

She let the comment pass. The front door of the house opened. A frail woman, who Thurber took to be Teresa Reilly, walked out. More accurately, the woman teetered out the front door and somehow managed to navigate the two porch steps without falling on her ass or spilling anything from the tall plastic cup she held. Tom introduced his wife to Thurber, who noted that the old man subtly moved between the two women, as if shielding his wife from her or vice versa.

"Mrs. Reilly, I was just explaining to your husband that I'm taking a new look at the accident that killed your daughter. I apologize if this brings up some bad memories but I want to be sure the previous investigation was thorough. Just wanted to let you and your husband know."

The woman moved slightly to the side so that her husband no longer stood between them. "My Pammy's dead," she said, her voice so slurred that Thurber barely made out the words.

"And I'm so sorry for your loss. I can only imagine how you must feel, even so many years later." She paused for a reaction, which Mrs. Reilly did not provide. Then she added, "I'm sure you and your daughter were very close."

"We were all very close," Tom answered for her. "Despite Ray's trying to shield her from us, we kept close."

"Oh, shut up, Tom!" Teresa said with remarkable clarity. "You and all your bullshit about Ray. About Pam still being alive. The psychics, the private eyes. Pammy died in an accident!"

"Teresa, please, maybe you should go back—"

"I talked to her the day before she died. Last time we spoke." The woman had the florid face of an inveterate drinker, her nose spiderwebbed with veinlets despite her efforts to conceal them with makeup. "We were going to have lunch that Friday. She called to say she couldn't make it. Goddamned company. Worked her to the bone."

Thurber waited to hear if Teresa had more. She did not, as if the recollection of that last conversation had transported her back to that day. The woman took a long drink from the plastic cup.

"Is this about the e-mails Ray's been receiving?" Tom said.

"What e-mails?" Thurber said.

"He didn't tell you?"

"No." Thurber's pulse sped up. So far her investigation hadn't yielded anything, the cryptic phone call she'd received the only new information in the case, a phone call whose veracity grew less and less credible the more she looked into Pam Courage's death. In both her conversations with Ray Courage, he'd not said anything about receiving any e-mails. When she approached him at the restaurant after he'd done something on his phone, he looked like a kid caught with his hand in the cookie jar. Had he been looking at an e-mail? Sending one?

"He came out two days ago to talk to us."

"Does he come to visit often?"

"No, not at all. It's been years since we've heard from him, let alone seen him. He said he received a couple of e-mails from Pam. I thought that's why you were here. To follow up on the e-mails."

"Tell me more about the e-mails."

"Ray said they came from Pam and that they accused him of trying to kill her, and that she was going to make him pay. Here I thought she'd staged her death, not that he'd actually tried to kill her. Bastard. The son of a bitch only came up here to tell us so he could find out if Pam had contacted us, too."

Tom's words stunned her. In more ways than one. That Courage withheld that information incensed her. She'd specifically asked him if he knew anything about the anonymous phone call she'd received. Surely an e-mail accusing him of murdering his wife would qualify. He hid that bit of information. And that made him look suspicious. Could Pam Courage still be alive? There had been a body, which could not be reliably identified as that of Pam Courage. Thurber had discounted the theory—whose only proponent had been Tom Reilly—that Pam still lived. This news at least opened up that possibility.

The e-mails to Courage, coupled with the anonymous phone call, proved nothing. She needed more. Short of finding the caller, which she held little hope of doing, she needed to go bust Courage's chops and get a look at those e-mails. More and more, she started to believe Pam Courage had been murdered. And somebody wanted whoever did it to pay.

thirteen

"The best you can do is Davis?" Lobo asked Jeffrey Colton, the recently hired NSA spook. Lobo and Root stood behind the man as he worked on his computer, four large-screen monitors occupying most of his desktop space. Each screen showed different data or documents, all indecipherable to Lobo. Myriad electronic gadgets littered the inside of the small office, some of which Lobo could identify as electronic eavesdropping equipment and GPS vehicle trackers. Most of the stuff, however, he had no clue as to their function. He just knew they were probably expensive. Colton liked to spend money on his toys. From what Lobo could tell, the money was well spent. Mastrov loved the results his new employee delivered. And if Mastrov was happy, Lobo was happy.

"UC-Davis to be a bit more precise, somewhere on campus." Colton looked less like a spy and more like a computer nerd, replete with thick-rimmed glasses, a collared, short-sleeved white shirt, and a short haircut straight out of the 1950s.

Lobo knew better than to judge Colton by his appearance, having seen the forty-three-year-old wizard accomplish more with a few keystrokes than an army of traditional leather-on-pavement security men could achieve in a month.

He'd done the background check on the man himself. IQ well north of 150. 2380 SAT score out of high school. MIT graduate with a perfect 4.0 GPA in computer science. Dropped out of the PhD program in advanced computer science at Stanford because he found it too easy and boring. He wanted a world of action, not one of academic abstractions and staff meetings dominated by gasbag professors. He signed on with the NSA after a fierce recruiting war for his services with the CIA, FBI and Homeland Security. His fifteen-year career with the NSA was marked with major achievement, but few promotions, his inferior social skills the primary cause of the flat career trajectory. This lack of recognition, despite his extreme capabilities, prompted Lobo to hone in on him as the ideal candidate to fill the surveillance position that Mastrov had instructed Lobo to create. The negotiations had proved surprisingly easy, Colton not reluctant to undertake jobs in the gray area of legality. The generous compensation package Mastrov offered squelched any concerns in that regard.

Upon his hiring, Colton's job responsibility list was short, consisting of a couple of dozen homes and offices to tap, and a few e-mail accounts to monitor, including that of a certain Ray Courage. In Courage's case, he was to look for any correspondence related to Pam Courage. That was it, the extent of his instructions. If any e-mails, texts or phone calls came in mentioning Pam in any way, Lobo was to be contacted immediately. Colton had done just that.

In terms of skills, Colton was the real deal. Lobo just couldn't figure out why they couldn't isolate the e-mail sender to a spot more precise than a five-thousand acre college campus.

"You can't nail down the location better than the entire campus?"

Colton explained something about servers and routers and other crap Lobo had no interest in. He glanced at Root who was working his jaw. Lobo reached over and touched Root's arm to calm him, not wanting him to explode at Colton.

"So far it's just been the three e-mails, right?" Lobo said.

"Actually, four. He got one a little while ago. But it doesn't say much. Courage sent her a message to stop bothering him. Here take a look." He opened the recent exchange between Courage and Pam1111. Lobo and Root read it and exchanged glances.

"I'm telling you, these e-mails are just someone fucking around with this guy," Root said. "That bitch couldn't have lived."

"Maybe she wasn't the one in the car," Lobo countered. "Or maybe she walked away from the accident." This he knew to be nearly impossible. He'd been there. No one walked away from something like that.

"No way." Root shook his head and folded his arms across his chest. "I'm telling you these e-mails are just bullshit."

Lobo felt inclined to agree with him, that the e-mails to Courage were intended to mess with him. Why someone would do that, he couldn't figure out. And that loose end bugged him. Fully accustomed to the "Crazy Zebra Way," Lobo felt confident that he had sufficient resources devoted on the Courage front. Belt and suspenders. Check and double check. Boots on the ground—Mastrov's term for directly engaging the enemy—this was the crafty CEO's way. There was no such thing as being too thorough. And Lobo had risen to his current stature with the company through a meticulous adherence to this philosophy.

"What about the bugs in his house and the tap on his phone?" Lobo said.

"Well, he did call his daughter and asked her if she'd received anything. She didn't, of course. I already knew that because I'm monitoring her e-mail as well. I put a GPS tracker on his car last night. Today he's been down in the delta to a place called Slager's Towing. Then he went to lunch. After that he went to a Dana Krabbe's house."

Again, Lobo and Root exchanged looks.

"Keep Ray Courage as your top priority," Lobo said. "It's got low probability of turning into anything but the stakes are too high. Even a one in a thousand chance is too risky. Keep me informed."

"Always," the spook replied.

Outside Colton's office, Lobo put a gentle hand on Root's shoulder and they stopped in the hallway leading to their respective offices. "I'm going to need you take a bigger role on the surveillance side of the Courage thing."

Root nodded.

"I've got my plate pretty full right now and I think you're ready to take on more responsibility." Lobo nearly choked on the words. He didn't like Root. More importantly, he didn't trust this man who had his own ambitions and agendas to fulfill. Mastrov liked him, though, and instructed Lobo to mentor Root. And, in all practicality, Lobo needed someone to monitor the Courage operation. He needed Root to step up.

Root, perhaps feeling a tinge of human emotion, spoke. "I know I messed up in Nevada. Should have wasted the guy in the desert after we had him dig his own grave. Just like we talked about. I got a little mad is all. Won't happen again. I promise."

"Okay," Lobo said. "Do me a favor and find out who's sending those e-mails to Courage. Something about that isn't right, and we can't have that ball of string unravel on us."

fourteen

I promised Rubia that I'd accompany her and Cuellar to the presentation at Miles Hunt Middle School in Sacramento that afternoon, so I sat with them in the school's main office waiting for our escort to the gym. Sitting on that straight-backed wooden bench, we looked like three students waiting for a scolding from the vice principal.

"You sure you don't want me to talk to the students?" I asked. "After all, I am a former professor of speech communication."

Rubia rolled her eyes. "A lily-white college professor walks into a room full of Latino ... stop me if you've heard this one before."

"So you're saying I lack the *ethos* to adequately persuade the audience."

"That's exactly what I'm talking about. *Ethos*. Geez! Cuellar, see what I've had to put up with."

Cuellar smiled and nodded. On the drive over we learned a little more about him. He'd come to Sacramento six months earlier, after living in Los Angeles for nearly twenty years. He was born in Houston, living there until sixth grade, when his parents moved so his dad could take a job at the port in Long Beach. He'd grown tired of the LA lifestyle, with its constant traffic jams, blighted streets, and high cost of living. The final straw, as he told us in the interview, was the gang-related shooting deaths of his two nephews. Two weeks after attending their funerals he moved to Sacramento, where he knew no one. I had checked his reference at the security company that employed him. The manager I talked with confirmed he was a good employee, currently working four days a week at various supermarkets around town as assigned by the company. His criminal history check came up empty, just as he told us during his interview.

"You play basketball?" Rubia asked him.

"Little bit."

"Ray and I play a game of HORSE once a week. If you ever want to play, let me know."

"Okay. I'm more of a soccer guy, though. Played four years in high school."

"You know, I've been thinking of starting an IML soccer club to give the kids something to do. Just haven't had the time, what with the bar and everything else I've got to do. Might be something I'd pay you to take on if you're interested."

"Maybe so," he said.

We lapsed into silence as we watched a handful of students come and go, presenting or receiving leave slips at the front desk. Funny, I thought, fully entrenched in the digital age and so many years removed from my own middle school days, the old paper leave slip system endured.

"What part of town do you live in, Cuellar?" I asked to make conversation.

"Over in Oak Park, in an apartment just off Broadway on 32nd. It's not very nice but it's all I can afford, for now anyway."

That was a particularly rough part of Sacramento. While Cuellar might have the size to take care of himself, I didn't know about his street smarts. He looked a bit more refined than the typical resident in that neighborhood.

A woman in a "Hunt Middle School" sweatshirt appeared in front of us, introducing herself as the principal's secretary.

"We're so thrilled to have you," she said, speaking at once to all three of us. "We're starting to see more and more problems and this year seems to be the worst. Having a program like yours can really help us keep these kids out of trouble."

She led us into the gym, a poorly lit, cold hangar that smelled like soup. In the back, three women in hairnets moved about behind the counter separating the school kitchen from the gym, apparently cleaning up after the lunch hour. Several tables with attached benches covered the back half of the space, while about a hundred metal chairs had been unfolded and set into rows facing a microphone stand at the gym's front. The basketball backboards had been raised up to the ceiling and a volleyball net was piled in the corner.

"The students will begin arriving in about five minutes," the secretary said. "We thought it best to split them into two groups, so you'll have twenty minutes with each one."

When the secretary left, Rubia turned to Cuellar and me. "I don't have a great feeling about this," she said.

"Why?" I asked. I already knew that she didn't like giving large audience presentations, preferring to meet in groups of ten to fifteen students, where she could engage them in a more conversational style and get to know their specific experiences, interests, and concerns. A large audience did not allow for that kind of give and take.

"You heard her say they thought it best to split up groups."

"Yeah so? Two groups should be better than one bigger one."

Rubia shook her head firmly. "No. You think I asked to come to this school at random? Uh, uh. I chose it for a reason. This school is right on the border between two of the baddest gangs in the area—the East Street Mob and Los Venenos. My bet is that they split the groups up by gang affiliation, not to keep the size of the room down."

"Maybe," I said. "But that's good, right?"

"I don't know. It could mean that the school people don't think they can control their own students."

We heard the students coming before we saw them, as loud and rambunctious as you would expect from two hundred seventh and eighth graders. They drifted into the gym in groups of two or three, engaged in lively conversations, punctuated by an occasional friendly shoulder push. The teachers did their best to herd them toward the empty seats. Rubia moved to the microphone as the first couple of dozen found seats, their conversations continuing. Cuellar and I went to the side of the room, our roles to observe and lend Rubia moral support. The teachers amped up the effort to seat the students and a couple of minutes later, one of the male teachers, most likely a PE teacher judging by his large stature and the sweat suit he wore, commandeered the microphone and silenced the crowd. He introduced Rubia, and she immediately launched into her presentation.

"How many of you here know someone who is in a street gang?" she asked, raising her own hand.

The students looked at one another, shrugging and nodding, until one student raised her hand slowly. A couple others followed suit, then a couple more, then in a matter of seconds everyone had a hand raised.

"Okay, thank you. I'm not going to ask how many of you are in a gang or who wants to be in a gang. I do want to tell you that I understand what it is like going to this school, living in this neighborhood, and the temptation to join a gang, sell drugs, carry a gun, the whole deal. When I was your age, I was in the same situation. And I gave into it. I joined a gang when I was thirteen years old. Thought I was badass. Thought I was cool."

"What gang were you in?" called out a boy in white T-shirt and slicked back dark hair.

"Doesn't matter. It was a gang just like the ones in this—"

"She's the sista ran Los Modernos. Badass bitch, man!" Another boy shouted, he too wearing the white T and the slicked back dark hair.

"Chinga su mama, ella es un mamacita." A third boy shouted, and the entire audience laughed.

"Silencio!" Rubia demanded. The volume of her voice over the microphone and the unbridled anger on her face quieted the room.

"You in the T-shirt." She pointed at the third boy who had called her a *mamacita*. "What gang are you in?"

The question seemed to embarrass him and he looked down to his lap.

"You don't need to answer because I know that you're in Los Venenos. I can tell by the T-shirt and your hair. And I bet you're wearing one orange sock and one red one."

I looked at the feet of the students in the audience and saw dozens of students with the mismatched socks Rubia described.

"Yeah, I ran Los Modernos. Yeah, I made money selling meth and smack. Yeah, I carried a gun. Know what that got me? Time in jail. My three best friends shot and killed. My mother disowned me because I shamed the family. If I'd been a gangbanger a month longer I would have ended up dead, too. True story."

As Rubia was talking, the voices of the students scheduled for the second assembly session could be heard outside the gym. One of the female teachers shut the door to dampen the noise.

"I'm not here today to tell you 'quit your gang' or 'drugs are bad' because you won't listen to me, at least not right away. What I am asking is for you to—"

The just-closed door burst open and several male students in plaid flannel shirts and black pants rushed in. Six or seven of the boys seated in the audience rose as one and charged at the gatecrashers. The cursing and yelling escalated quickly into a maelstrom of flying fists.

Rubia, Cuellar, a handful of teachers, and I tried to break up the bedlam. I stopped a fight between two boys by standing between them, an extended hand on one boy's chest, my other hand on the second. To my right two girls started punching a third. I released the boys to break up that fight, and the two boys resumed their battle. The teachers, even the burly PE coach, fared no better than I in stemming the melee.

I looked over at Rubia. She and Cuellar, the only calm ones in the room had already ushered out the majority of the students, the ones not engaged in the fighting. Now they systematically broke up the violence, a fight at a time, by roughly forcing the combatants to sit on opposite sides of the gym. I took my cue from them and attempted the same with the three girls.

As I escorted away the girl who'd been targeted by the other two, I sensed something to my left. I looked up in time to see a student about to strike me with a metal chair. Out of nowhere Cuellar leapt in, grabbing the chair in mid-descent. He then flicked it aside, and in one motion, had the boy by the wrist, wrenching it behind his back and forcing the kid into submission on his knees.

A man-sized student came to help his friend, throwing a punch at Cuellar's face. Rubia's new assistant reached up with his free hand and caught the fist less than six inches from his face. He repeated the maneuver he'd executed on the first boy. Two seconds later, both boys kneeled helplessly on the gym floor. The gym teacher came over and led one boy away. Then the other. By now all fighting had stopped. The teachers had ushered everyone out of the gym, presumably the gang members well separated from one another to prevent another flare up.

In a matter of a few minutes, Rubia and Cuellar had restored order. The choreographed action looked like they'd been breaking up school fights together for years. I knew then that Rubia had the assistant she needed. Unfortunately, that did little to salvage the disastrous turn of events

I walked to Rubia and said, "Might have been your best speech yet. When's the next gig?"

She glared at me.

fifteen

Glorified penguins, so goddamned hip, you go girl, right the ship!

Claire had not driven down the street in years, the old mix of adventure and anticipation joining her like old friends as she slowed to look for signs that the street still offered the treasures she'd found here as a teenager. Sometimes they would stand on the corner. Other times they'd come out after she drove up and down the street three or four times. They'd come out soon, the BMW drawing them out like kids to an ice cream truck playing an insipid jingle.

Jingle jungle, Uncle Jim, kill the bastard, murder him!

God, remember that? She used to sing that one to herself every day. Even on the days he didn't touch her. Five years of therapy had not erased it after all. The recollections assaulted her. Put up the shields, she commanded herself, part of the stupid visual imagery she'd been taught. Stupid, but it usually worked.

No signs of anyone, either out on the street or at the house. The neighborhood looked pretty much the same. Lower middle class, the place you'd find mechanics, store clerks, truck drivers, and bartenders. Respectable people, who kept their yards tidy and cars washed. People who minded their own business. The house looked like all the others, though the occupants consisted of a gang of teenagers and men in their early twenties. She parked in front of the yellow house with the faux baby blue shutters, deciding to stay no more than five minutes if no one came out.

She pulled down the driver-side visor and slid open the mirror cover. She liked her new hair color, maybe a bit too black compared to her natural dark brown, but not too bad. The black eye makeup might be a bit much. Too Goth. Not the look she was going for at all to start her new life. She'd experiment to make it look right. Even so she looked good. The guys still ogled her. The guys. Fucking pricks. All they wanted was one thing. Use. Abuse. Repeat. God, how she hated them.

For a second, doubt crossed her mind about the wisdom of revisiting this habit of her past. No, just this once. To celebrate. Turning twenty-one. The automatic boost to her trust fund, up from the ridiculous amount she'd had to scrape by on the past three years. She felt so great for once. Empowered like she'd never felt before. Her plan was working. Plus, she could get her singing career going for real, show everybody that she did have talent, that she would be famous some day.

Sophie Carter, Lily Brown, little bitches, mow them down!

Just when she put the car into gear to leave, the door to the yellow house opened and a small Hispanic man dressed in a plaid flannel shirt and black pants walked out to her car. She rolled down the passenger-side window and he leaned in, not a man at all, a boy no more than fifteen years old.

"What you want, mama?" he said, his street Mexican accent no doubt the result of hours of practice.

"A half gram," Claire said. She'd come for a quarter, but what the hell. It's just this once, so live a little.

"*Aye chi mama!* Gonna cost you two bills."

"Is it good stuff?"

"Straight from Columbia." He pulled out a baggy from his pants pocket and showed it to her inside the car.

The baggy looked to have about the right amount. And the quality had never been at issue here before.

"You want to taste it first?"

He meant go inside and shoot some up. She had no desire to do that. Little punk would try something. She shook her head. With her left hand, she reached down to the space between her car seat and the door, getting a firm grip on the kitchen knife she'd brought along for protection.

"Open it up," she said. When the boy parted the top of the baggy, she released her grip on the knife, reached over with her right hand, stuck the long fingernail of her pinky inside and scooped up a sample of the heroin. She brought that to her nose and snorted it skillfully. Oh, yeah.

Rukie dukie, Kalamazoo, Haleiluhua , boop de do!

Fifteen minutes later she returned to her childhood home. She still hadn't gotten used to living here again after all the years being away. First with her aunt and her scumbag husband, then two and a half years at boarding school. Her mom left instructions in her trust to rent the place out until Claire turned twenty-one, giving her daughter the option to move in or to continue renting out the place. She could not sell it under terms of the trust until she turned thirty. She didn't mind that. The Greenhaven neighborhood house trumped the dumpy apartment she'd occupied the past three years. It would feel like home again soon, though she wondered if she would shake the sadness she felt when she first walked through the door two weeks before.

Then her world changed again. Finding the old boxes in the garage was like seeing her mom all over again. Seeing her handwriting, touching it, knowing that her mother had touched that very same paper. She spent days going through all her mom's things, mainly work documents and files. In one, she found her mom's appointment book and read the note clipped to it on the last day of her mom's life. That explained everything. Impulsively, she'd called the cops, her excitement overcoming her judgment.

She sat at the kitchen table, everything she needed in front of her. The old ritual came back to her like riding a bike. That made her laugh. When was the last time she'd ridden a bike? She'd probably fall on her ass. The heroin melted and bubbled in the spoon from the heat of the butane lighter. She filled the syringe and found the vein in the crook of her elbow without needing to tie off. She winced as the needle first pricked her, soon relaxing as she watched herself ease the liquid into her vein.

She went to the living room, turned on the music, plopped down on the couch and stretched out. The days ahead would be the turning point for her, the start of a new life. Fulfilling, blissful and complete. Kurt Cobain sang to her and her mind drifted away.

The last clear thought that swam into her head before she slid into nirvana—*Mommy dearest, killed too soon, not to worry, I'll slay the goon.*

sixteen

The late afternoon sunshine slanted dimly through the window blinds of Dr. Ernest Gray's tiny outer office, casting the room in a dull gray. A yellow Post-It Note on a door that I assumed led to the inner office read "With a patient. Please take a seat."

I tried to switch on a floor lamp next to the window. Nothing. A doll-sized table lamp sat atop a short bookcase. Flicking that on did little to overcome the growing darkness. Between the lamp and a cube of facial tissues sat three certificates in separate plastic prop-up frames. Taking a closer look, I saw that the frames contained Gray's yellowed college degrees, which included a BS and MS in psychology from California Lutheran University in Thousand Oaks, California. He earned his doctorate in psychology from the University of San Francisco some forty-seven years before, which put Gray somewhere near eighty years old.

I ventured to sit on the threadbare and stained red couch, testing it first with a finger to make sure none of the stains were recent enough to rub off. If a patient came here depressed, nothing in Gray's outer office would serve to mitigate the feeling.

The bookcase held two shelves, divided in the middle to form four quadrants, each with an apparent target audience in mind. The two bottom quadrants contained books for kids, the left for toddlers, the right for elementary and middle schoolers. The top left shelf probably aimed for his female clientele with at least twenty books on relationships, feelings, having it all, and understanding men. The last subject could probably have been best addressed by looking at the top right shelf, clearly targeting men with tomes on sex, beer, wine, and sports. I reached over and pulled out a biography of former baseball player Moe Berg, who, after his fifteen-year Major League career, became a spy for the United States' Office of Strategic Services.

Just as I was cracking open the book, the door from Gray's office opened and out walked two women, one about forty, the other in her late teens, likely mother and daughter. They did not appear happy, the teenager storming out two steps ahead of mom, whose sad eyes revealed a profound hopelessness.

In their wake, Ernest Gray appeared, a spry, ebullient man beaming with good will as he extended his hand in greeting.

"Mr. Hancock, right!" he said with gusto.

"Actually, no," I said as we shook hands. "It's Courage. Ray Courage. I called earlier today."

"Courage, of course. How could I forget a name like that? Bravery, guts, spunk . . . Courage! I like it!"

"Thank you," I said, not knowing how else to respond.

"Come on inside." He led me into his inner office and took a seat in a tan leather chair, its arms patched with duct tape. Behind him stood a row of a half-dozen metal filing cabinets. I sat opposite him in a blue love seat straight from the 70s. Between us lay a throw rug that might have been white at one time. To my right was an end table, on which sat yet another cube of facial tissue. Either his patients had allergies or they cried a lot.

"Now then, what can I do for you, Bob?" he began. He reminded me of a squirrel, the nervous little movements, eyes darting about. Wasn't much bigger than one either.

"Ray."

"Yes, of course."

"I guess I should just jump into it. And I know it will be a long shot—"

Gray caused me to stop speaking when he loudly pulled the tab of an aluminum can to open it. "V-8?" he asked, gesturing towards me with the can.

"No thanks." I wasn't sure where he'd found the can. Maybe he had them stored in the folds of the leather chair.

"I love this stuff." He took a long, satisfying drink.

"Anyway," I continued. "I was wondering if perhaps my wife came to visit you, you know, professionally. It would have been thirteen years ago."

"What was your wife's name?"

"Pam Courage."

"Tall drink of water with brown eyes and a nice figure? Sure, I remember her."

"No. I don't think that's her. My wife was medium height and had blue eyes." I let the reference about the woman's figure pass.

"Even if I did remember her, I'm not allowed to divulge anything about my patients," he said, before adding in a stage whisper, "It's about doctor-patient confidentiality."

"I understand. It's just that this is very important. On the day she came to see you, if she did come to see you, she was killed in an automobile accident. I'm trying to understand what was going on that day, to learn if something was bothering her."

"Ah, you're looking for a clue. How fun!"

"I guess you could say that."

"Are you sure you don't want a V-8? I just love them."

I shook my head.

"I'm not recalling anything about your wife. Pat did you say it was?"

"Pam."

"Yes, of course."

This was getting worse by the minute. I tried a different angle. "How about a Dana Krabbe? You saw her several times back then. Maybe you remember her?"

"Tall drink of water with brown eyes and a nice figure?"

Oh my god. "No, Dana is none of those things. Not to be rude, but Ms. Krabbe is quite heavy and has several medical disorders, including a case of psoriasis."

He scratched his chin and took another swallow of V-8. "My memory isn't what it used to be."

Really.

"Do you happen to know anything about why this woman would have come to see me?"

"Not really. It might have been something to do with her medical problems. You know, how to deal with them mentally. That kind of thing."

"I get a lot of those."

"She worked for Crazy Zebra Empires. She saw you using their EAP program."

"Crazy Zebra, hah! Love that name! Love it! Yes, I did work for them under contract back then. I was one of their EAP providers. Saw quite a few of their employees, as a matter of fact."

"Do you remember Ms. Krabbe, then?"

"Tall drink of—"

"No, remember she was heavy and had psoriasis."

"Yes, of course."

"That does seem vaguely familiar to me now that you paint the picture for me. Her skin sort of flaked off. And she was a smoker. You could smell it on her when she walked in the door. Most unpleasant odor, cigarette smoke. You don't smoke do you?"

"That sounds like her," I said, ignoring the question. "If my wife Pam came to see you it would have been a referral from Dana Krabbe. They worked together at Crazy Zebra."

"Crazy Zebra," he said, chuckling. "Wonderful name."

"Did Dana Krabbe refer my wife or anyone to you?"

Gray looked over his shoulder at the file cabinets. "Like I said I really can't tell you much about my patients. If I did that nobody would come see me. And I'd lose my license."

"How about this, then. How about you just check your files to see if my wife ever came to see you. You won't have to reveal what you talked about. Just whether she came here." If he found my wife's file, I'd worry about accessing its contents later.

"I do have all my Crazy Zebra EAP files on hand. My policy is to never throw anything away. You never know when it might come in handy."

"Like now, for example." I figured a little nudge wouldn't hurt.

"Yes, exactly!"

The old guy bounded out of his chair and went to the filing cabinet to his left, setting the beloved can of V-8 on top. He put on a pair of reading glasses and started in on the file cabinet. He mumbled something to himself as he looked through the top drawer, then the second. When he opened the third drawer, he said, "What did you say your wife's name was again?"

Patience, Ray, patience. "Pam Courage."

"Yes, of course." He shut the drawer and went to the filing cabinet at the other end of the row. He spent several minutes looking through three drawers of the second cabinet before declaring, "Nope. No Pam Courage."

I don't know which I felt more, surprise that he'd remembered the name, or disappointment that he'd not found her.

"You sure?"

"Found your Krabbe, Dana. But no Courage."

I thanked him and began to leave, disappointed and a bit miffed that I had wasted so much time with Dr. Ernest Gray.

"You know, she could have gone to another therapist. There were four or five us contracted with Crazy Zebra's EAP program back then. We referred patients to one another all the time. Especially if they called and needed to see someone right away. If we had a full calendar, we'd send the patient off to someone else. That happened a lot." He giggled.

"Do you know who the other therapists were back then?"

"Oh, my. So long ago. No." He stopped and thought for a moment. "Wait a minute. Let me check something. He riffled through the files in the bottom drawer of the cabinet and produced a single sheet of paper. "Here we are. An e-mail from Crazy Zebra's HR Department titled 'Declaration of Policy Change Regarding EAP Remuneration.' It was sent to all of us nearly fifteen years ago." He began to read the e-mail to himself. "Buncha malarkey. But see here," he said, his eyes fixed on the sheet. "It was addressed to Amanda Bennett, Christopher Marshall, Scott Davies, myself and Susan Whitehead. That was all of the EAP therapists accepting their employees at the time."

"Do you know if they are all still practicing?"

"Heavens no. I would have no idea. I practically pulled a brain muscle finding this memo." He shook the e-mail at me in case I'd forgotten what he was referring to. "Besides, we didn't really know each other. We were just contractors to the same company but we each ran our separate practices."

I jotted down the four names, hoping I might be able to catch at least one of them before they closed down for the evening.

seventeen

"Why don't I just waste the sorry-assed rat and do it a favor," Root said.

"Leave it be," Lobo replied.

"Barking's driving me crazy. Yippee little thing."

Lobo had herded Dana Krabbe's Chihuahua into the bathroom and shut the door, which got it out of sight if not earshot. For twenty minutes the creature barked away and Lobo was tempted to let Root put it out of its misery. He resisted doing so, not so much because he cared about the dog, but because he didn't want Root to get his way.

"Place is a dump," Root observed. "There's crap everywhere. Smells like an ashtray. Who can live like this?"

Lobo couldn't argue that point. The place disgusted him as well. They'd swooped in minutes after Krabbe had left for what he'd hoped a quick errand. Now he worried she might have set out for something more time-consuming, like a doctor or hair appointment. Based on his observation of the woman earlier, either one of those might require a lengthy procedure.

They stood in the kitchen wearing latex gloves, their feet covered with paper booties. Even with the gloves they touched nothing, not that either of them wanted to. Lobo stood far enough back from the kitchen window to remain unseen from the street yet close enough to see a car pull into the driveway.

"You think this bitch told Courage something?" Root asked.

"Nah, she doesn't know anything. At least not enough to be a

84

problem."

"Ain't going to matter, anyway."

"Nope," Lobo said. He admired his plan. Though he hadn't told Colton all the details, he could tell the former NSA pro had been impressed. He kept Mastrov uninformed about the operation, standard operating procedure to protect his boss with a shield of plausible deniability.

Fifteen minutes later, Krabbe's car turned into her driveway. The two men moved to the door between the utility room and the garage, listening as the car pulled into the garage and the car's engine stopped. The garage door rumbled to a close and a moment later, the large woman entered the utility room.

Root sucker-punched her in the right temple. For a second she stood, stunned, eyes blankly focused ahead, before she stumbled forward two steps and dropped to the floor. Root smiled at the sheer power contained in his right fist.

"Why'd you hit her? Now we have to wait for her to come out of it."

Root shrugged, the smile still on his face.

Krabbe came to after Lobo tossed cold water onto her face a few moments later. They sat her in front of the computer in a corner of her living room. Gagged, and bound at the feet, her eyes bugged in terror at the sight of the two men standing on either side of her. She tried to talk, the resulting noise a wet convulsing nonsense. Snot streamed out her nose.

"Shut. The. Fuck. Up!" Lobo commanded. "Look here, Ms. Krabbe, this is going to be very easy. You won't be hurt if you follow my instructions.

She gave a slight nod. Her entire body trembled.

"Log into your computer and get into your e-mail account."

Her hands shook so badly she could not steady them over the keys. Lobo wanted to backhand her himself, but that would make matters worse. "Please try to calm yourself. The sooner you do what we say, the sooner we will be gone and out of your life forever. Then you can go about your business like none of this ever happened."

She nodded again. Despite her persistent trembling, she managed to enter her username and password to open her Gmail account. Lobo then gave her Ray Courage's e-mail address and commanded her to type it in. Next, he dictated word for word the message he wanted her to send. When Krabbe finished typing, Lobo leaned in to make sure she had entered the words correctly:

> *Mr. Courage,*
> *I promise not to tell anyone what we talked about*
> *yesterday. Your secret is safe with me. You didn't have*
> *to threaten me to stay quiet. I've known for a long time*
> *that you did it. Please just leave me alone and I will*
> *never bother you.*
> *Dana Krabbe*

Lobo considered changing the message to add something explicitly saying that Courage killed his wife. He rejected that because it might elicit an immediate response from the man. He didn't want that. For his purposes, the message, as is, would be enough. Satisfied, he told her to hit send. She dispatched the e-mail before turning with hopeful eyes to Lobo.

The dog continued to bark in the bathroom. A couple of more hours until darkness would help cloak their departure from this rat hole. Two hours listening to that damned dog, cooped up in here with this disgusting woman and Root.

"Get up," he told Krabbe. With her feet bound together, the woman lacked the strength to hoist her considerable frame from the chair, struggling to do so two or three times.

"Help her up," he instructed Root.

"No, I'm not touching her."

"Don't be a little girl. Besides you have gloves on."

Lobo cut the plastic tie around her ankles. "Put her in there with the dog. That'll shut it up and get her out of our way. Then bind her feet again." He handed Root a second plastic tie.

Reluctantly, Root did as told. The dog shut up and he could barely hear the woman, who had started whimpering in route to the bathroom.

"Okay, let's finish staging this scene," Lobo said. "Once it's dark we take her out of here."

Earlier in the day, inside Courage's house, they found an empty beer bottle with fingerprints all over it, which they presumed to be his since he had not had a visitor in the days they'd been monitoring him. As an extra bonus, in the wastebasket next to his computer, they found a small slip of paper with Krabbe's name, phone number and address written on it.

Root took both items out of a brown shopping bag. First, he took the beer bottle and threw it against the fireplace, breaking it into dozens of pieces. Next he placed the slip of paper on the coffee table between an ashtray and a box of Cheez-Its.

Lobo nodded approvingly. "That should do it."

"Now what?"

"We wait till sunset then get down to Locke. I told Slager we'd meet him about six-thirty."

eighteen

I sat in the back office of the Say Hey, the bar starting to fill with patrons taking advantage of happy hour. Except for completing and turning in my workers comp report and video, the day had proved fruitless. The offices of the two therapists I visited after seeing Dr. Gray were already closed for the day. None of the EAP psychologists I called that evening answered their phones.

I did a Google search for Pam Courage, looking for images that might have been used to create the likeness sent to me by Pam1111. To my surprise I found three photos of my deceased wife. One photo in an old *Sacramento Magazine* showed her with three other women at a charity fundraiser. Another was the obituary photo I'd sent to the San Jose State Alumni Magazine. The third photo, a head shot accompanying an announcement of Pam's promotion to finance manager at Crazy Zebra, could have been used to create the animated photo sent to me if the perpetrator had a decent knowledge of graphics software.

November mid-afternoon crowds were sparser than those in the spring, the Say Hey, understandably, more of a baseball bar. NFL football games drew pretty good numbers, especially on Monday and Thursday nights. When the NBA Sacramento Kings played, patrons stood three deep at the bar, every table in the small space filled. The Kings played the Lakers tonight, which would mean another full house. I hoped to be long gone by tipoff. I reread the e-mail on my laptop yet again:

*You say you meant no harm to me. How can I believe
you? You set in motion some bad things. I'm not sure
how to react to your e-mail.*

I hit the "Reply to Sender" icon to open up a window for my
response. For twenty minutes I typed and deleted, typed and deleted.
Again, the identity of the sender influenced the message so
dramatically that I couldn't find the right message or the right tone to
use. God, could it be Pam? I longed for her so badly, a longing that
pulled at me harder than ever as I imagined that she might be alive.
Pam, Sara and I back together. No! I could not open that part of me.
You don't go thirteen years remembering her each day, but especially
birthdays, wedding anniversaries, and the day she died, without
building an emotional callous, one thin layer at a time. You don't do so
intentionally. On the contrary, as much as it hurts, you want the pain to
be as sharp years later as it had been on Day One because somehow it
makes her life more real, not a fading memory, a real person with a
heart and soul you loved in every cell of your body. Nature builds that
callous as a way to protect us from our unwillingness to let the pain
ease away a day at a time; if it didn't, such an intense pain endured for
so long would kill us. If I believed hook, line, and sinker in Pam's
living, I would rip off that callous. If Pam lived, her presence would
replace the pain with the deepest love, the richest joy. But if it turned
out she had not come back to me, I feared the realization might destroy
me. I could not risk that. At least not yet.

"Geez, Ray, you look like that statue, the one with the naked guy
pondering the universe." Rubia walked in with two pint glasses filled
with a reddish beer.

"What are you talking about?"

She put the glasses down on the table, sat down across from me,
and then put her fist under her chin, elbow on table. "You know, this
statue."

"The Thinker by Rodin?"

"Yeah, that's it. The Thinker. Only thing I've ever seen a naked
guy think about is—"

"Okay, okay."

"Anyway, you seem very serious about something. Still thinking about the e-mails?"

"Yes," I said, then spent ten minutes telling her about the latest correspondence between myself and Pam1111, and the visit the day before from Lieutenant Thurber.

She thought for a moment before speaking. "Looks to me like you could be getting set up."

"That thought occurred to me, too. It doesn't make any sense, though."

"Who would benefit from you being convicted of killing your wife?"

"That's the thing. Nobody would."

"Come on, Ray. Think about it. The answer is never nobody."

"There's only one obvious possibility—except for my loony ex-father-in-law. Did I tell you he's believed that Pam never died? That she faked her own death to get away from me? When his daughter died it drove him farther around the bend than he was before. And it tore up his wife even more, sent her crawling into a gin bottle."

"You don't think he's behind this?" Rubia said, holding her glass of beer up to the light to inspect it.

"I mean it's possible, but no, not really."

"Which leaves …"

"The only person who would benefit from framing me for Pam's accident would be the real person who killed her. That makes no sense, though. Because, first of all, the police don't know who did it. They never even developed anything close to a viable suspect. By now, the trail to the other driver has got to be a stone-cold dead end."

"And that's what you're doing now, right? Trying to find the trail. The Thinker man, Ray Courage."

"Are you going to give me one those beers or what?" I asked.

She slid the second glass towards me while she sipped on hers. "Tell me what you think of it."

I took a sip of the beer.

Rubia awaited my reaction. "Well?" she said.

"Good," I said. "What is it?"

"It's Ruhstaller 1881 Red Ale. I'm thinking of ordering a couple of cases a week."

I nodded in approval and drank some more.

Our friendship went back several years now. We met on her first day of college, where, she told me later, she felt woefully out of place, entering my classroom, eyes wide, and freezing with fear two steps in. Because it met graduation requirements and served as a prerequisite for other classes, my "Introduction to Public Speaking" class tended to attract freshmen and sophomores. The young woman standing just inside the doorway of my class that day looked older, not so much chronologically as much as in the depth of her eyes, the way she looked about the room searching for danger, and the way she carried herself. Despite her fear of this strange environment, and her instinct to bolt, she did not do so. I watched as she selected a seat in the front row of my class. Five minutes later during roll call, I learned that her name was Rubia.

On the second class session of a semester, I have students interview a fellow student, then introduce them to the class. The exercise helps students get to know one another and also practice their public speaking. We had an odd number of students that day, and Rubia ended up without a partner, so I paired up with her. I told her my story and she told me hers. She was born in West Sacramento to teenage parents who worked minimum wage jobs to provide for her. The dad became an alcoholic by the time Rubia turned ten and left for parts unknown. After that her mom could not control her. Despite pleading, tears and a couple of interventions by her extended family, Rubia could not be stopped from running with a street gang that sold drugs, enforced their territory with violence, and extorted protection money from small businesses. By the time she turned eighteen she ran the gang. Busted at twenty-one for a reduced charge of possessing a controlled substance, she decided after nearly three years in jail to quit the gang life, get a college degree, and live life on the straight and narrow. Released from state prison thirty days before, Rubia's journey towards a new life had just begun in my class.

Over her four years at Sacramento State I became her chief confidant, helping her navigate the arcane halls of academia. I wept at her graduation ceremony. When she inherited the Say Hey I volunteered to help in any way that I could, not because I'm a right on kind of guy, but because in my entire life I have never met anyone so honest, so true to herself, and who was such a good and loyal friend as she. That day in class, when we told each other our stories, changed my life.

"Wish I could afford to hire Cuellar full time," she said. "He's really smart."

"And good in a dust-up," I added.

"That, too."

"I think you have the hots for him."

"You think I have the hots for any male under the age of thirty-five, with chiseled features and an athletic build."

"There you go."

"I have standards," she said.

"Never said you didn't. Merely suggesting that once the standards are met, then it's Katy bar the door."

"What the hell does that mean, 'Katy bar the door'? How old are you, a hundred and ten? Katy bar the door." She shook her head.

"Hilarious." I drank more beer.

"You know, with this e-mail stuff going on and all, I think you should pack."

"A gun?"

"No, a lunch. Yes, a gun."

"You know my feelings about that."

"Yeah, liberal ass academic doesn't believe in guns."

"Guilty."

"I could get you a nice Glock, same as mine for a really good price and—"

I held up my hand to stop her. "Besides, you shouldn't be carrying a gun with your record."

Someone in the bar called for a bartender. Rubia stood to go serve her customers. "All I got to say about that, professor, is that I'd rather be an alive ex-felon with a gun, than a dead ex-felon without one."

Once she left I turned back to the e-mail and started to write.

*You asked how you can believe me and that you are
unsure of how to react to my e-mail. That is exactly
how I have felt after receiving your messages. So, if
you are indeed Pam, as you claim, where did our first
kiss take place? What college class did we take
together? What cafe did we go to every Sunday before
our daughter was born?*

*If you can answer these questions, then you might
actually be my wife. In that case, I would implore you
to meet with me in person so that we can clear the air
about what you think I might have done.*
--RC

Fifteen minutes later I started to log off my laptop when a new e-mail arrived. The response from Pam1111 startled me:

RayRay,
*Your questions are insulting. Let's not play a game of
Ray Courage Trivial Pursuit. However, your
proposition does intrigue me. Let me think about it.*
Pam

She avoided the questions, just as I thought she would. No surprise there. The "RayRay" did surprise, the nickname she called me by. Was this Pam's way of saying that it was really she, while refusing to let me control the conversation with my questions? Or, was it one of a number of people who heard her refer to me by the nickname years ago?

Most of all, I sensed a subtle shift in tone, the vitriol of the previous messages easing a bit. The writer's willingness to consider my proposition to meet gave me a measure of hope that I'd soon learn her true identity.

nineteen

Mastrov strode through the lobby of Crazy Zebra Empires like the emperor he was. He insisted on casual dress for all his employees, so when he walked among them, he alone wore a business suit—this one made in New York for twelve thousand dollars—that relegated the be-jeaned and T-shirted minions to peasants in the presence of his superior attire and invincible reputation.

To his right, a few dozen employees enjoyed a free late afternoon snack in the company's three-star cafeteria. On his left, an employee received a company-paid haircut, while in the neighboring space, three employees received massages. Just as he passed the indoor basketball court, a golf cart replete with a clothes rack carrying several stacks of laundered garments zoomed past. Another Crazy Zebra employee perk.

The big man stepped outside the headquarters building to a glorious afternoon. Huge billowing clouds hovered above and beyond the river to his left. He took in a deep breath of the cool, fresh fall air. Heaven. He turned back to look at the office he had personally designed—not at the paper and pencil level—but at what the architects had called the "programming" stage, a fancy term for what he wanted the building to be like for himself and his workers.

His building stood only three stories, Mastrov did not believe height dictated quality, or power or strength, but its footprint on the east side of the river just north of downtown Sacramento rivaled that of the Sacramento State University campus. The headquarters building served as home to twenty-eight hundred employees, with another eight hundred employees residing in six other buildings scattered among the oaks and pines in the pastoral setting. In all, Crazy Zebra Empires covered three hundred acres along the Sacramento River, an empire that Mastrov planned to keep growing. Not only did Crazy Zebra own the largest parcel of land of any company in Sacramento County, it was also its largest private-sector employer, taxpayer, and contributor to causes ranging from homelessness to spousal abuse support shelters.

He treated his employees well. The best facilities. Perks that rivaled those of the Googles, Yahoos, and others down the road in Silicon Valley. He paid well, too. Mastrov never understood CEOs who garnered seven, eight and even nine digit annual incomes, but who insisted on limiting employee salaries in the name of cost control. Good salaries bought you good employees. More importantly of all, it usually bought you loyalty, the characteristic Mastrov desired most in his employees. For key employees it was a requirement, which if found lacking meant severe consequences.

About a quarter mile from headquarters, he entered the smallest building in the complex, one only a handful of men had access to. He punched in his seven-digit code, then put his thumb on the touchpad for a bio identification. Thirty seconds later he entered the office of Jeffrey Colton.

Colton reacted with noticeable surprise at the sight of his employer. Mastrov had spoken with the man twice—at his hiring interview and when he welcomed him into the company, a perfunctory event for executive hires or, as in Colton's case, highly specialized employees.

The former NSA specialist technically reported to Lobo, as it should be. Over the years Mastrov learned to delegate better, something he found difficult to do at first, his penchant for perfection instilling a micro-management mentality. As his empire grew it became impossible for him to keep track of each and every aspect of his operations. He hired top executives from around the country, luring them away from some of the best companies in the world with huge salaries and performance bonuses they could not refuse. Employees in his human resources department came from the most progressive organizations, creating a company structure, reporting and compensation systems that attracted applications from tens of thousands of potential employees each year. As a result, Crazy Zebra could be very selective, hiring only the smartest, innovative, and hardest working employees in the world. As guided by Mastrov, these employees built a health, fitness and entertainment powerhouse that began to rival the likes of Nike, ESPN, Adidas, and Sky Sports. His 24-hour Crazy Zebra Empires Network, or C-ZEN, grew faster in revenue and ratings the year before than any sports network ever.

Smarts, good people, and progressive management keyed the success of his company. What he learned as a fighter held true in business—always maintain your competitive advantage. And that meant hiring people like Colton to keep tabs on the competition and to put out fires when they flared up. When it came to his prized former NSA employee, Mastrov couldn't resist the temptation to circumvent the chain of command and talk to this underling directly. Besides, Lobo and Root were out in the field today and he didn't want to wait for the information.

"Lobo has updated me on some of your work lately. I have to say that I'm impressed."

"Thank you," Colton said, bowing his head. He had stood when Mastrov entered the room. "You make my job easier with all the resources you've provided."

"You keep producing the results you have so far and you'll keep getting the resources." Mastrov pulled up a chair and sat opposite Colton. "Please sit down."

Colton sat, having to use a slim space between two computer monitors to maintain eye contact with the boss.

"What are you working on now?"

Colton hesitated, fully aware that protecting Mastrov at all costs meant not divulging anything illegal or incriminating to him personally or his company.

"You can speak in generalities," Mastrov said, noting the man's reluctance.

"Okay." He let out a breath of air. "I'm tracking the whereabouts of … um … a person of interest."

"The one receiving strange e-mails from an unknown party?"

"Correct."

"Has this person gone anywhere or done anything that appears troubling to you?"

"I'm not sure."

The answer did not surprise Mastrov. Colton could not know what to look for. He'd been instructed to monitor Ray Courage's e-mail and phone conversations for any mention about Crazy Zebra or Pam Courage. He'd received no context for the monitoring or any instructions beyond communicating his findings to Lobo.

"He's visited a towing company down in the delta, his wife's parents, and a middle school. Today he visited a psychologist named Ernest Gray."

"Why did he do that?" Mastrov asked.

"Not sure. He set up the meeting with a phone call, but he didn't say why he wanted to talk with Gray."

Mastrov pondered this a second. "Make sure Root is apprised of this. Anything else?"

"There have been more e-mails."

"From this anonymous sender?"

"Yes, and he's sent a couple out as well. He sent one a few minutes ago and she responded."

"So they are engaged in a dialogue."

"Not really a dialogue," Colton said. "The messages have been short. The subject is trying to figure out if the person is who she says she is. And I think he wants to meet with her."

"Has anything been set up?"

"No."

Mastrov raised his eyebrows. "You'll let Root know if they do arrange a meeting. He'll need to make sure he's there to intercede."

The former fighter rose to his feet feeling pretty good about the state of his security operations. "Have you heard anything from Lobo on the operation with that woman?"

"You mean—"

Mastrov cut Colton off with a raised finger before he could utter a name. "You know what I mean."

"Yes. In fact they are at her house right now."

"Perfect," he said. "Perfect." Just the way he liked it.

twenty

Just before dinner, darkness already settled in, someone knocked at my door. Demetrio Gutierrez stood there sheepishly when I opened the door. He'd been to my house twice before with the rest of his family, once for dinner and another time to watch a World Cup match.

"I don't mean to bother you," he said, his voice lacking its usual confident energy.

"Do you want to come in?"

He shook his head. "I just came to thank you for all you've done for me. And for Lucinda. Without you, we would not be going to Buckingham on scholarship. Who knows where we'd be right now if we had to go to the high school by the house."

"Don't be silly. You and your sister are smart. I didn't do anything but show what was available. That's all. Is that the reason you came all the way out here? To thank me?"

"No, but I didn't want to forget it because I also appreciate your help with the college applications, all the visits at the colleges. Everything."

I put up a hand to stop him. Enough with the compliments, anybody with half a heart and an eye for academic talent would have done the same thing.

"So, I wanted to tell you in person that I'm not going to apply to any of the colleges."

"What? Don't say another word. We need to talk about this." This time I insisted he come inside. He followed me into the kitchen, where I'd been making chicken saltimbocca and a green salad.

"Have you told your parents?"

"No." He sat at the kitchen table while I chopped a red bell pepper for the salad.

"Do they know you're here?"

"Yes. I told them I needed to talk with you some more about the college applications."

"Okay, tell me what's on your mind."

"I've decided it would be best if I stay here in Sacramento and go to City College."

I stopped chopping. "Look, Demetrio, City is a great option for a lot of students, especially those who can't get directly admitted to a decent four-year school and want to transfer. Or students who can't afford university tuition. But you have so many more options, great options. You can't let those slip away."

"I wouldn't fit in at any of those schools, especially Occidental. All those rich kids, all from the best neighborhoods, with their fancy cars, they'd just look down at someone like me. Barrio Boy."

"Hello. Barrio Boy. You happen to go to The Buckingham School, the snootiest school in the entire area. Last time I drove past the student parking lot it was filled with BMWs and Mercedes. I even saw a Ferrari. You get along with them, right?"

He nodded.

"They don't look down on you do they?"

He shook his head.

"There you go. If anything, college students are going to be more accepting of people from different backgrounds. Don't worry about that."

"I just don't think I can cut it in college. It will be too hard. I'm not smart enough."

"I'm not going to do the GPA and SAT run-through with you yet again," I said. "I was a college professor and I didn't even know what you and that Oxy neuroscientist were talking about when we were on campus. He was salivating at the chance to have someone with your intellect and academic curiosity on his research team. So don't give me 'not smart enough.'" I resumed chopping the bell pepper and moved on to green onions. "Have you eaten yet?"

"No, sir."

"Let your parents know that you're eating with me, then. I'm making more than enough for the two of us."

In the kitchen, I placed a chicken breast on each of the plates, then spooned some sauce over each one, adding a sage leaf as garnish just for the hell of it. Demetrio set out knives and forks and placed the salad bowl and serving utensils on the table.

"Look, if you don't want to apply early decision that's fine," I said as we settled into our seats. "But you need to apply to all your schools."

"I don't know," he said after he finished chewing a bit of the chicken. "It costs so much money. The Occidental website said tuition, room and board, books and everything will cost sixty-four thousand dollars a year."

He was grasping for every excuse he could come up with. I wasn't about to let him do that. We'd stay here all night if we had to, him finding excuses not to go to college, me shooting them down. "You heard as well as I did that your parents wouldn't have to pay a cent for you to go to Occidental. Same would be true at pretty much every school on your list. Between your parents' income, your grades, and test scores you've got a full ride coming somewhere."

"This is really good, Mr. Ray," he said, not acknowledging the veracity of my words.

We ate in silence for a while and I could tell he was searching his personal lists of why going to a four-year college was not for him. I'd seen the same reticence in students at Sacramento State whose parents had never attended college. They'd ultimately enrolled in college but only after overcoming their fears and insecurities of being the first ones in their family to do so.

"I don't know. Southern California is a long ways away. Even Berkeley is almost two hours by car. I've never been that far from my family. I'd get homesick."

"Skype, e-mail, texting," I said, putting down my fork and counting out each method of communication on my fingers.

"Telephones, Amtrak, Greyhound, and Southwest Airlines. And they go both directions," I concluded, holding up seven fingers.

"I've heard you need a car in Los Angeles. That you can't get along without one."

"How'd you get here tonight?"

"The bus."

"Rumor has it that Los Angeles has buses and a light rail system."

"I wouldn't be able to look out for my sister."

"Okay, I understand that, but even if you go to City College there's no assurance that you'd be able to walk her home every day. Besides, I think Lucinda can take care of herself. And you need to set an example for her. If you go to City, she'll probably follow you there. Show her that you have the determination to attend one of the best schools in the country and she'll follow in your footsteps. She looks up to you. Show her the way."

We both finished our dinners. I refilled our water glasses with the pitcher on the table. I held up my glass and said, "Here's to you going away to college."

He didn't agree, but he didn't argue either. He did clink glasses with me and that seemed like a good sign.

"Let's finish up here," I said, starting to clear the table. "Then I'll drive you home."

twenty-one

Claire parked her BMW in a large parking lot next to the Activities and Recreation Center on the University of California, Davis campus. Darkness had already fallen as the bells from the center of campus chimed seven times.

She pulled out a gray backpack from the rear seat of the car, more a prop than anything, all the better to fit in as one of the disgustingly bright-eyed and eager students on this campus. This place made her want to vomit, with its Disneyesque vibe, the bubbly kids riding their little bicycles with their precious backpacks and all too cute clothes paid for with mommy and daddy's credit cards.

Too cute for words, too stuck up all day, do us a favor and just go away!

She trudged, backpack slung over one shoulder, from the Recreation Center towards the middle of campus. She crossed the bike path near a roundabout, and a male bicyclist wearing headphones nearly crashed into her, swerving violently to avoid her. He stopped, ripped off the headphones, and told her to watch where the fuck she was going.

"Fuck you!" she yelled and began charging at him. The kid's eyes widened and he tore off before Claire could reach him.

She breathed heavily, from the combination of exertion and anger. Not smart, she told herself, looking around to see if she'd drawn the attention of anyone. Cool, cool. Sometimes her anger got the better of her. She needed to watch that. Blend in, don't stand out, bitch.

By the time she reached the quad a few minutes later, she felt considerably calmer. To her left, a couple of dozen students sat at tables inside a well-lit building with floor-to-ceiling windows. The students focused their attention on something that Clair could not see, her view blocked by an interior wall. A speaker? A television mounted on the wall? A moment later she heard what the students had been anticipating as a funky bass beat joined a retro rock drum mash and an old school punk guitar riff brought the small crowd to its feet. Claire felt a surge of excitement, deciding to delay her work for just a few minutes.

Music, music, beat inside, take me for a magic ride!

Inside, she could tell the band members were students, the drummer and bass player sporting de rigueur tattoos. The lead singer, a chick with pink and white hair, lacked the all-in commitment of her bandmates, eschewing the tatts, opting instead for piercings—tongue, cheek, nose, and ears. Bunch of posers. The chick started to sing the lyrics to a classic 80s song. Her voice lacked style or any passion for the music. Claire stood behind the audience and watched them finish the song. She turned to leave when the band started another song, this one a soulful ballad from the 70s. Again, the stupid chick butchered the song. As an artist, Claire couldn't take it anymore. She started to sing.

The song called for the instruments to play soft and low so that the singer carried the song on the strength of her voice. The girl with pink and white hair, even with the benefit of a microphone, could not match Claire's roaring voice at the back of the room. The audience turned to look at her. Claire felt a surge of pride, elation, and redemption. These people loved her as she knew they would.

"Shut up," a guy yelled. Probably the girl's boyfriend. Claire kept singing.

"You wacko, quiet down and show some respect," said a particularly repulsive-looking girl.

"Knock it off," said someone else. "At least learn to sing before you act so rude."

Claire kept singing, though by now the band had stopped playing.

Before long, the entire audience had turned on her, shouting insults. They began tossing food and paper plates at her. Claire stopped.

She raised both her arms in the air and gave them a double-barreled finger salute as she mouthed "Fuck You." She then gave an elaborate bow before exiting the way she came in.

"That's why I never went to college," she said to herself as she continued across the quad. "Bunch of stupid ass kids don't know dick."

A five-minute walk later, she entered the library, less populated now than in her earlier visits, most students probably back at their dorms or apartments for dinner. On the third floor she had her choice of several open desktop computers. From the backpack, she pulled out a sheet of paper on which she had written the user ID and password. She put up an ad on Craigslist under Gigs>Computers and less than an hour later she met some kid named Tyler who was more than happy to exchange a UC Davis user ID and password for $200. Claire suspected he'd ripped it off someone else rather than sharing his own log in information with her. The little shit then tried to hit on her. Fucking guys.

Once she logged on to the system, she opened a browser window. First things first. The short article in the *Sacramento Bee* from five years ago:

> *Sacramento Man Killed in Hit-and-Run Accident*
> *A 45-year old man was killed yesterday in what police*
> *called a hit-and-run accident. The victim, James*
> *Miller, was struck by a vehicle while apparently*
> *jogging down Primrose Way, a quiet residential street*
> *in east Sacramento. Miller lived three blocks from the*
> *accident scene. A witness heard the accident while*
> *preparing dinner inside her home. She said the victim*
> *was lying on the sidewalk with no cars in the vicinity.*
> *Miller was transported by ambulance to Mercy*
> *Hospital, where he died from internal injuries shortly*
> *after being admitted. Police are asking anyone with*
> *information about the accident to call 916-555-4300.*

Claire smiled. Whenever she needed to have her confidence pumped, reading the article did it every time. Short and sweet, no fawning copy over the bastard. Barely even a mention in the newspaper, more, really, than he deserved.

Her inbox had four promising additions since she last checked, all responses to her e-mail request to audition for some of her favorite bands. She opened the first one, a rejection of her request, a form rejection no less. The second e-mail turned her down as well. So did the third. And the fourth. At least they had the decency to reply to her e-mail, she consoled herself, unlike the all the others she contacted.

Over at Craigslist she reread her ad:

> **Lead Singer Looking for a Band**
> *Female vocalist (think Florence Welch!) seeking rock and roll band to front. Must have paid gigs already scheduled. Contact Claire.*

So far no responses. What the hell? Wait until she takes some band platinum, then everyone will feel so stupid for missing the chance to work with the next Janis Joplin.

Several hours had passed since their last e-mail exchange, long enough for him to sweat whether she'd respond at all. Time to set the trap on the man who killed her mother. Her mom's note in her datebook couldn't have been clearer. Ray Courage killed his wife. But first he killed her mother.

In a new browser window she logged into her blastermail account, typed in his e-mail address and crafted her message:

> *Okay RayRay, I would like to meet with you. I still don't trust you but am willing to give you a chance to explain yourself. How about we meet on the 17th at 9pm? There's a statue called "To The Pioneers" just behind the Sacramento Zoo on the north side. Will meet you there. Come alone or I will not show up.*

Three days should be plenty of time to get everything together. *Creepy man, dirt bag, full of lies, get ready now for a big surprise!*

November 15

twenty-two

Lobo entered the tilt-up industrial building on the seedy north side of Sacramento, half-surprised to find Dana Krabbe still alive. Root had drawn the unwelcome assignment of watching her overnight in the cold, dank warehouse. Lobo thought his capricious employee might terminate his confinement with the woman by wasting her for the sheer fun of it. That would have spoiled the plan, though Lobo had a contingency in place, just in case. Maybe Root's impulse control was improving after all.

"Put her in the car," Lobo said, nodding at the woman's car parked inside the building.

"Want me to cut her loose?" Root said. Krabbe's feet and hands were bound and she still had the gag stuffed into her mouth.

Lobo nodded and watched as the bindings were cut and the gag removed. "Don't say a word or try anything," he said to her. "If you do, my friend here will shoot you. If you follow instructions you will be fine and you'll be back home with that little dog of yours by afternoon. Now get up."

She'd spent the night seated in a plain wooden chair. From the looks of her, she'd been sobbing, though by now fatigue had set in and she had stopped her protestations. Both men walked her to the rear of the car. Root popped open the trunk and gestured for her to get inside.

"Where are we going?" she said weakly.

"Just for a little ride," Lobo said.

Root drove the car towards downtown, Lobo behind him in the

106

Challenger, sunrise still a good ten minutes away. For some reason, Lobo felt nervous about the operation, though so far it had gone flawlessly. Maybe it was all the moving parts in this one, the human elements. That's where things could go wrong and bite you. They merged on to Interstate 5, Root in the lead proceeding at an inconspicuous sixty miles per hour, just as Lobo had instructed. A new storm front had come in overnight and a torrent of rain battered Lobo's car. Spray from several big rigs in front, and to the side, hindered his visibility even more. He was relieved when they pulled off the freeway and drove through the park to the adjoining residential neighborhood.

Lobo continued to follow behind Root as they slowed in front of the house before continuing on. Lobo picked up his cell phone. "Looks like he might still be home. I'll wait just up the street and keep an eye on the house. You wait in the park and I'll let you know when he's gone."

Lobo fretted over the next step, the one that would be most risky—getting Krabbe into the damn house unseen. Root had checked out the neighborhood the previous morning and reported that all the nearby residents left for work by eight fifteen in morning. As eight o'clock approached, several people had already departed, their homes darkened, clearly vacant until they returned home in the evening.

The rain started to ease, slowing to a light drizzle before stopping altogether. Hazy sunlight sifted through the blanket of clouds to the east. Two cars drove by, neither paying him any mind. At eight o'clock, Ray Courage walked from his front door to his car in the driveway and drove away. Lobo opened the GPS tracker app and watched the progress of Ray's vehicle. Once Courage had merged onto I-80, Lobo figured he would not be returning to the house anytime soon. None of the adjacent homes, or the ones next to those, appeared to have anyone inside at the moment. It was time. Lobo texted Root: *Let's go.*

Three minutes later they had hustled inside Courage's house, Lobo working his magic on the lock, then taking a final look around neighborhood as Krabbe and Root went in ahead of him. He searched for the computer, finding a desktop PC in a home office down the hall. He had instructed Root to put on their standard latex gloves and paper boots. Now, he did the same. As he'd hoped, they had gotten inside quickly enough so that the computer hadn't locked up. Colton had provided the log on information to him anyways, but this would save even that step. Courage's e-mail account was opened and Lobo noted that he'd opened the e-mail from Krabbe, sent the day before. He had not responded to it. Good. Very good.

It only took a few seconds for him to spot the e-mails from Pam1111. He deleted all of those. Next he deleted the e-mails in the "Sent" folder to Pam1111. Once that was completed he cleared the "deleted" files. A thorough forensics sweep could uncover and retrieve the existence of the deleted e-mails. Removing them might keep the police in the dark about their existence, preventing them from looking for the e-mails at all. The Krabbe e-mail should trump any need to look further. Even if they did, the Pam1111 trail would lead nowhere.

The calendar on the computer contained a few entries, but did not appear to have a comprehensive listing of Ray's meetings or appointments. Lobo knew for certain that he'd visited Larry Slager and Dana Krabbe two days before, though he'd not entered them into his calendar. Lobo typed their names into the calendar at the approximate times of Courage's visits the day before. It took all of five minutes for him to complete the necessary work on the computer and return to the living room

Krabbe sat terrified on a large sofa in the living room. Tears streamed down her cheeks and her body shook severely. Root looked at the street in front through a partially opened wooden blind.

"We're cool," he declared to Lobo.

Lobo paused for a minute to think. He went over everything between when they had broken into Krabbe's house until this moment. Check. Check. Check. He smiled. "Then I think we're good to go," he said.

Root nodded in reply before pulling out his pistol and shooting Krabbe three times. Twice in the chest and once in the back of the head, the coup de grace, delivered from point blank range.

twenty-three

At eight in the morning I left home for the office of Amanda Bennett, one of the psychologists whose names Dr. Gray had provided. Part of me said to abandon the entire psychologist thread, yet something prodded me on. Dana Krabbe's assertion that Pam sought out a psychologist on that last day needed to be resolved one way or the other.

Dr. Bennett's practice occupied an office in a sprawling one-story complex on Cottage Way just off of Watt Avenue. I checked out her website the night before, learning that she'd been practicing for nearly twenty years and had an undergraduate degree from the University of Nevada, Reno and a doctorate in counseling psychology from the University of Oregon. Her listed hours of operation were from eight thirty in the morning until five in the evening, Monday through Friday. I hoped to catch her before eight thirty, when I suspected her first patient might arrive. When I tried her office door about eight fifteen I found it locked.

"Can I help you?" came a woman's voice behind me.

Amanda Bennett looked very much like the photograph on her website, though she was taller than I expected. My first reaction was that this might be Dr. Gray's elusive "tall drink of water," though I didn't think my current unscheduled presence was the right time to broach the matter. I took her through the situation, much as I did with Gray the day before. To my surprise she demonstrated no resistance or skepticism to my story. She even seemed to find some sympathy for

109

me. She unlocked the door and we entered. She punched in the key code to turn off the alarm system, then toggled a switch on a second panel next to the alarm pad. "Security cameras, inside and out. We've had vandals and break-ins so I leave them on overnight."

She hung her coat on a wall-mounted coat rack and turned up the thermostat.

"I'm assuming that your wife authorized you under the Health Information Privacy Act to have access to her medical records, right?" She wanted me to say yes. In truth, I couldn't remember if Pam and I had done that or not.

"Yes," I said.

"Good. Since the HIPPA forms from back then sometimes got misfiled I won't bother to verify that. Your wife's records wouldn't be in my computer. They're too old. We didn't convert our old records of non-recurring patients into our new system. I'll have to look at the paper records to see if she was a patient of mine."

She excused herself and entered the second of two doors down a short hallway. A few minutes later, she returned carrying a manila envelope. "I'm sorry, but it doesn't appear that your wife was ever a patient of mine." She opened the folder and pulled out several stapled sheets of paper. "This is the master list of all Crazy Zebra patients who came to see me that year. Your wife isn't on the list."

Another dead end.

I returned to Dr. Christopher Marshall's office, this time finding it occupied. Unlike Drs. Gray and Bennett, Marshall had an actual reception area and a real-live receptionist, a perky young blonde who greeted me with a way too cheery "Good morning!". She then informed me that Dr. Marshall was with a patient but would be available briefly in about a half hour. Perky and I spent the next thirty minutes drinking coffee as I learned about her lifelong ambition to star in the Sacramento equivalent of the show *Cake Boss*. While not exactly riveting, it was a pleasant enough way to while away half an hour. The time, unfortunately, was not well spent as Dr. Marshall also confirmed that Pam had not been a patient of his at any time. He was able to shed some light on why I couldn't find Dr. Susan Whitehead during any of my web searches.

"I believe she died several years ago," he said. "Shame, really. She had a drinking problem. I only knew her a little bit and knew that. Being in our profession you'd think she would have sought help."

Yet another dead end.

At ten o'clock I figured I had time to try Dr. Davies since his office was in downtown Sacramento, and on the way to my eleven o'clock meeting with Rubia in West Sacramento. As I drove, I thought about the e-mail that Dana Krabbe had sent me the night before. Very strange. Our visit had been pleasant enough, a little creepy, but pleasant enough. Her e-mail made it sound like I had threatened her or something. I wondered if, on top of all her other maladies, she suffered from the overindulgence of alcohol, which had caused her bout of paranoia. Either that or something or someone scared her into thinking I posed some kind of threat. I had called her last night and when she didn't pick up, I left a message for her to call me back. If she didn't call me, I would need to double back to her to find out what was going on.

If I suffered from depression, anxiety, mania, obsession-compulsion, panic attacks, social anxiety, ADD, separation anxiety, or any other mental disorder, Dr. Scott Davies would be the therapist for me. I didn't know if he was any good at his profession, but boy did he look like a therapist. Mid-forties, with a slender athletic frame, a full head of wonderfully coifed gray hair, and a golfer's tan, he looked like a young Peter Graves. His reassuring demeanor and mellifluous voice came straight out of central casting as well. I could envision him starring in his eponymous TV show, *Dr. Scott Davies, Licensed Clinical Psychologist!* Cue upbeat theme music.

Alas, as good looking and reassuring as he was, the SOB didn't have squat for me about Pam, either, officially making the morning a waste of time.

I made it to the IML office ten minutes early. For budget reasons, Rubia settled for a former auto repair service station in a less than enviable part of West Sacramento, where her neighbors consisted of a Vietnamese nail salon, a Korean massage parlor, a Mexican mercado, a Hmong hubcap and tire wholesaler, and an American Goodwill Industries. It was a veritable United Nations of commerce.

Rubia spoke into her cell phone as she sat at one of the old metal desks she'd bought at a salvage yard.

"We would love to present to your class," she said. "No age is too young, but fifth and sixth graders are ideal." She listened for a few seconds to the person on the other end of the conversation. "December fifth at nine o'clock would be perfect. I'll see you then."

"You booked another speaking engagement?" I said.

"You're on your game today."

"I'm sure the glowing reviews you received from Miles Hunt Middle School sealed the deal for you. Nothing like a full-on riot to make friends and influence people."

Rubia chuckled. "Man, seeing you in the middle of that scene still makes me laugh. Thought you was going to take that chair up the side of the head."

"Thank goodness for Cuellar."

"Amen to that."

I recognized the kid as soon as he walked in a few minutes later. He may have added a couple of tattoos to those that ran from wrist to neck on both arms, but otherwise looked the same. On a cold, rainy November day he wore the same baggy black shorts, white wife beater, and straight-brimmed Detroit Tigers ball cap as he had in March. Back then he'd helped me with his computer skills to bypass the log in and password to access a laptop. His help played a big factor in solving that case.

"Hey," I said in greeting, a smile breaking across my face.

The kid's hangdog expression did not change. If he recognized me, he showed no sign of it. He looked at Rubia, or rather he looked at Rubia's feet, as he spoke. "CK said you needed me."

I remembered now that he never gave us his name, only to contact CK if we needed him again.

"How much to track an IP address on an e-mail?"

"That's it?" the kid said. "You could do it yourself."

"Yeah, and I could change the oil in my car myself, but I'd rather pay someone to do it," Rubia said. How much?"

"Fifty bucks."

She looked at me and I nodded. That would be a bargain for finding out the location from which Pam1111 was sending her e-mails.

"I can't get you down to a home address or anything like that. If it's from a company, I couldn't know which exact computer was sending the e-mails. There could be proxy servers. And the ISPs don't release that kinda information to anyone but the cops, and even then they need a subpoena. But I can probably get you a pretty good geolocation."

Damn. The kid turns into Stephen Freaking Hawking once he starts talking computers. I handed him my phone.

"It's opened to my e-mail account," I said. "I want to see where the e-mails from Pam1111 are coming from."

He scrolled down through the e-mails in my inbox. Then he scrolled up through the e-mails in my inbox. After repeating the process a second time, he looked at me. "I'm not seeing any e-mails from nobody named Pam1111."

I took the phone back. He was right. What the heck? I hadn't deleted any e-mails in days, let alone those. A quick scan of the top thirty e-mails confirmed that the only ones that had been deleted were those from Pam1111. Could the sender have recalled the messages? No, that couldn't happen, especially after I'd already opened them. I opened my Sent folder, certain I'd find my outgoing messages. Again, no luck, the only deleted messages those to Pam1111. The Deleted Messages folder—same result. Clearly, someone had hacked into my computer, and I had no idea as to who or why.

twenty-four

Lieutenant Carla Thurber swore non-stop on the drive from the police station to Ray Courage's house, lights flashing, siren blaring, as she punctuated each epithet hurled at Courage by banging her palm on the steering wheel. She blamed herself for not acting sooner. After visiting with Courage's in-laws, she should have done something last night instead of telling herself to wait till morning. She had already worked a twelve-hour day, she had told herself, and she didn't have anything other than her suspicions to go on. He'd lied about the e-mails, but that wasn't enough to arrest him for a thirteen-year-old case where all the physical evidence had long since disappeared.

She stopped in front of the house, ducked under the crime scene tape, and approached the lead officer, who was standing on the porch out of the drizzle that had resumed.

"What have we got, Steve?" she said.

"Dead body on the sofa. Three gunshot wounds, two in the chest, one in the back of the head. CDL in pocket IDs her as a Dana Krabbe, sixty-six, lives across town."

"Who called it in?"

"Guy walking his dog called at eight twenty-one. Said he just heard what sounded like gunshots coming from the house. Officers Walters and Nickerson rolled up at eight twenty-nine, got no answer when they knocked, noticed the door was partially opened. When Walters stuck his head in, he saw the victim on the sofa."

"Where's the guy with the dog?"

"We don't know."

"I don't like that answer," she said cautiously. "And I don't like that look on your face."

"We have the 911 tape of the call. It lasted all of ten seconds. The guy just says he was walking his dog, heard gunshots, gave the address, and said to hurry. Then he hangs up. No name or nothing."

"What about the phone number. Who owns that?"

"Throw away."

"Shit!" Thurber slapped her thigh with her hand. "There's a lot of that going around. You're sure it was a man's voice." She wondered if it could be the same person who'd called a few days earlier about Pam Courage.

"Yeah, I listened to the tape myself."

Not wanting to leave the scene, she called the office and requested an arrest warrant and a BOLO for Raymond Courage, adding that he might be at the Say Hey on Broadway. From the sound of things, though, she doubted he'd be hanging out at a bar. The scenario suggested that he shot Dana Krabbe for some, yet unknown, reason, then in a panic, fled.

"He's got a daughter in LA from what I understand," she added on the phone. "See if we can get a number for her to learn if she's heard from him."

Thurber spent the next hour and a half directing the crime scene investigation team in their evidence collection activities. She told them she wanted a report with screenshots of everything on Courage's computer by three that afternoon. The living room, aside from the covered dead body sprawled on the sofa, looked as it did a few days before, during her evening visit.

She remembered Courage's car parked in the driveway that night, not uncommon in these older neighborhoods with smaller garages usually filled with too much junk to accommodate a car as well. With the door ajar, as Walters and Nickerson had found it, then it made sense that he ran out the front in a panic towards his car, in too much of a hurry to make sure he closed the door.

From the crime scene she drove to Krabbe's residence, where she met another investigator, Detective Pat Popejoy. She and Popejoy didn't always get along, he a disciple of Detective Lewis and five years her senior. His version of an ideal police department would be white, male, and over the age of fifty. Or in other words, a department of Pat Popejoys. A locksmith joined them and unlocked Krabbe's front door.

Immediately after entering the house, she could see that, in addition to the squalor of the place, someone had shattered a bottle, likely a beer bottle, against the fireplace. On the coffee table next to a box of Cheez-Its she found a note with Krabbe's name and address written on it. She checked the answering machine, the message indicator showing no incoming calls had been recorded.

As they moved through the rest of the house, nothing else seemed particularly out of place until they arrived at the hallway bathroom, where upon opening the door she found a Chihuahua, the source of the non-stop yipping that was giving her a headache.

Popejoy drove away just after the crime scene investigation team arrived. As Thurber approached the team to give them instructions, an older woman from the house next door hailed her.

"Excuse me, excuse me," the woman said. "May I ask what you're doing?"

Thurber showed her badge and identified herself as Sac PD.

"Has something happened to Dana?"

"I really can't say at this point," Thurber said. "May I ask your name and when was the last time you saw Ms. Krabbe?"

The woman said her name was Gloria Clark and that she had lived next door to Dana Krabbe for twenty-two years. She proceeded to provide a remarkable, if tedious, oral history of Krabbe's life, including when she retired, when her husband died, and when she adopted her Chihuahua from the SPCA. When asked if she had noticed any recent visitors at the residence, Ms. Clark did not hesitate.

"Yes, day before yesterday. A very good-looking middle-aged man came by in the afternoon. Dana never has visitors so I was quite surprised."

Thurber pulled out her cell phone and brought up a headshot of Ray Courage she had downloaded earlier in the day from his Sac State days. God, she loved the Internet.

"Do you recognize this man?" she asked the woman.

"That's him! Like I said, very good looking."

She was starting to get that feeling, tingly and warm, when things started to come together in a case, when the facts started to align, when loose ends started to tie together. "What about yesterday? Did she have any visitors yesterday?"

"I wouldn't know. I was visiting my grandkids in Loomis."

"Okay, if you think of anything else, please call me." Thurber handed a business card to the woman. "Oh, and wanted to ask you a favor. Would you mind looking after Ms. Krabbe's dog?"

"Steven Tyler? Sure, I don't mind at all. I love that little guy."

"I'll have an officer bring him over in a few minutes."

"Does that mean Dana won't be coming home for a while?"

"Yes," Thurber said before turning to leave.

Back at her office, Thurber sat at her desk and scrutinized the screenshots of the e-mails the crime scene team provided. The e-mail from Krabbe to Ray, sent the previous evening, looked particularly incriminating against the private investigator. The message sounded very much like he visited her to keep her quiet and threatened to harm her in some way if she said anything. Krabbe's line of "I've known for a long time that you did it" was not clear or conclusive, but it suggested that she meant Courage's involvement with his wife's death. Thurber had learned by phone on the drive over that Krabbe worked with Pam Courage at Crazy Zebra Empires up until she died in the car accident. Had Pam told Krabbe that she feared her husband? Or did she have some other kind of proof? Courage had called and talked with her for about a minute last night. Whatever he said more than likely induced Dana Krabbe to visit early the next day.

Next she looked for the e-mail Ray had received, supposedly from his wife. Pam's dad had said that Courage had visited on November 12, having received the e-mails on the eleventh. None of the e-mails he received on the eleventh made any reference to Pam Courage, the automobile accident or anything remotely connected to either. She looked through all of his messages before and after the eleventh. Nothing. She picked up her desk phone, punched in a four-digit extension.

"Hey, Tom, can you check the deleted messages on Courage's computer, starting with November the eleventh? I'm looking for anything that might be related to his wife and her death. Anything that might look suspicious at all."

She hung up and began drumming the fingers of her right hand on the desk as she pondered everything she had. Regardless of what she did or didn't have on the old case, the Krabbe case was coming together nicely. She felt confident she could establish the motive, means, and opportunity to build an airtight case against Courage. While she considered how to package it all for the District Attorney's Office, her desk phone rang. It wasn't CSI with an update on the deleted e-mails but rather the front desk.

"Call for you."

"Take a message," Thurber said.

"I think you'll want to take this one?"

An hour later, she sat at a cluttered workbench inside a decrepit garage in the middle of nowhere talking with a man with an alcoholic face and disagreeable personality.

"Okay, Mr. Slager," she said. "Let's go through it slowly this time, starting with his visit, and then let's work backwards. I want to get this one on tape." She set a palm-sized digital recorder between a stack of papers and an inverted truck piston-turned-ashtray. "Okay, go ahead."

"Like I said, this guy—"

"Ray Courage."

"Yeah, Ray Courage, he comes here unannounced the other day and he threatened me to keep my mouth shut if anybody—especially the police—comes asking about him."

"Why would he say something like that to you?"

"I didn't have no clue what the fuck he was talking about. Then I kind of remembered him. Been a long time. I says to him, you're the guy rented one of my rigs back a few years, right?"

"What did he say to that?"

"He nodded and said that's what I need you to shut up about."

"So he agreed that he rented a truck from you, and that you were not to tell anybody about it."

"That's what I said." Slager spit a dark brown stream onto the cement floor of the garage. "I told him, hells bells, I wouldn't of even

118

remembered you if hadn't shown up here. He said just keep forgetting about me or something bad could happen. Then he stares at to make sure I got his point."

"And what was his point?"

"That he'd fucking kill me. You could tell it from his eyes."

"Okay, let's move on. You say you remembered him eventually. When did you see him before?"

"I couldn't remember. I mean, I rent to a lot of people, but it had been a long time. So I went through all my old records. Took me awhile but I finally found it. He rented a towing rig from me thirteen years ago on November 11. Hold on." Slager sorted through the stack of papers and selected a yellow carbon rental receipt. He handed it to Thurber.

"See there," he said. "Says right there he rented a truck from me. Got his name, address, and driver's license number right on it."

Thurber nodded. Whatever had slammed into Pam Courage that night had been big. Big enough to drive away from an impact that had totaled her car and caused it to burst into flames. Something big like a tow truck for big rigs. She couldn't believe her good fortune. Everything was coming together almost perfectly.

"Once I looked at that agreement, it got me to thinking, and I remembered when he returned the truck it had some front end damage, even though it had a big ass piece of steel welded to the front. You can see on the form there I wrote 'returned with front end damage.'" Slager pointed to the notation at the bottom of the receipt. "I told him it would cost a thousand dollars to repair it and he didn't blink an eye and agreed to pay it. I think he just wanted to be done with the whole business."

"What whole business?"

"You know renting the rig and fucking it up. He just wanted to pay and be done."

"Did he say at the time why he wanted to rent the truck?"

"No, and I didn't ask. He gave me cash up front so I didn't care."

"Do you have a photo of the damage he caused?"

Slager spit again. "Nah, didn't have cell phone cameras back then and I didn't have a regular camera neither."

"What about a receipt from the shop that did the repairs?"

"Did the work myself," Slager said, smiling. "He paid that in cash, too, so I pocketed his thousand for myself. Turned out to be a nice pay day."

"So tell me, why did you call the police about the visit from Ray Courage?" Thurber glanced at her recorder.

"First of all, the motherfucker threatened me. I don't like that. Then it got me to thinking about why he didn't want me telling anybody about him renting my rig."

"Go on."

"So I get on the Internet and find out a little about him. One of the search results for his name turned up in an obituary in the *Sacramento Bee* for a Pamela Courage. And I saw that she died on November 11, the same day he rented my truck. Then I found an article on the twelfth about an accident on River Road, the one she died in, and it all just seemed suspicious. You know, him renting the truck, the truck having damage, her dying in a hit-and-run accident. That's when I decided to call the police."

"Well, we appreciate your sense of civic duty, sir." Thurber switched off the recorder, rewound it a few minutes, and hit play to make sure she got the testimony on the record. She then lifted the receipt by one corner and lowered it into a plastic evidence bag.

Only one thing could make the day even better—finding and arresting her one and only suspect.

twenty-five

Rubia left to work at the bar, leaving me alone in the offices of IML, my mood growing more sour by the minute. I called my Internet service provider. After waiting on hold for nearly a half hour, I connected with a customer rep whose accent was so thick she might as well have been speaking her native Hindi language. By the time we came to a reasonable understanding of each other, it was only to confirm what I already guessed—the deleted e-mails were irretrievable. And no, my e-mail was not "violated" according to my exotic-speaking new friend.

I wasn't sure of the significance of the loss of the messages, nothing in their content held a magic key to the sender's identity, be it Pam, Santa Claus, or Jimmy Hoffa. The mere fact that someone had come in and deleted my personal messages made me feel so, well, violated. Even worse, I knew someone had done so for a good reason, a reason for which I couldn't even venture a guess.

The entire psychologists' effort proved fruitless. And I doubted Dana Krabbe could be of further help. I thought for a minute or two about what to do next. The only logical choice seemed obvious. I found the number online and punched it into my cell phone.

A voice recording, thanking me for calling Crazy Zebra Enterprises, greeted me. I skipped the various options offered to me and pressed the "0" key. The company operator connected me to a woman who answered, "Office of Mr. Yuri Mastrov."

I asked to speak to the man and told her my name. Less than ten seconds later, the woman returned to the phone to inform me that Mr. Mastrov was unavailable. I asked her to have him call me back. I doubted he would.

As soon as I hung up the phone, the song *La Bamba* began playing. Rubia hadn't been amused that I'd picked the song of a talented Hispanic singer, Ritchie Valens, for her ringtone.

"What's up?" I answered.

"You may be in trouble, Ray."

"Oh."

"Yeah, you know the guy who delivers my Sierra Nevada order every week. Anyway, he delivers over at Tower Cafe, too. He was dropping off twelve cases of pale ale—can you believe that? Twelve cases? I only order five. Twelve—"

"Can we get to the part where I might be in big trouble?"

"Oh, yeah. Anyway, he says that these cops had just come from the Say Hey, but left because we weren't open yet. So, instead they come over to the Tower and start asking the manager and some employees if they'd seen this guy. They passed around a picture. It was you, Ray. They showed it to the Sierra Nevada guy and he recognized you right away."

"Well, I do take a flattering photograph, if I do say so myself."

"Don't mess around, Ray. This could be serious, the cops looking for you and all."

"Did he say why they were looking for me?"

"No, but there were four of them. They don't send four cops out to sell you tickets to the policeman's ball."

"There's a policeman's ball?"

"Ray, knock it off. You need to do something."

"Like what?"

"I don't know. Think of something."

We ended the call. Though I'd tried to sound flippant, Rubia's news stunned me. I didn't know how it connected to the disappearing e-mails, but I knew it did. Yeah, I know, brilliant. So brilliant that it sounded like the police would haul me away before I knew what hit me, how it hit me, or where it hit me.

This time my normal ring tone sounded. Caller ID showed it to be my lawyer, Mark Scofield.

"This isn't about my fantasy football team is it, because I can assure you I report all my earnings to the IRS," I said.

Mark ignored the banal attempt at humor. "Ray, did you know the police are about to arrest you?"

"As of about ten seconds ago, I was starting to get that impression, yes."

"I was in judge's chambers on a pre-trial conference this morning, when two detectives come in with an arrest warrant request. For *you*."

"Why do they want to arrest me? This is crazy."

"They found a dead body in your house this morning. A woman named Dana Krabbe. She was shot three times. They said you'd been intimidating her. The cops think that she came over to confront you, then you panicked and killed her. Ray, what is going on?"

"I really don't know, Mark. What should I do?" Panic started to set in. Everything seemed to be closing in around me. I walked to the front window of IML and looked to see if the police might be there. Not yet.

"Where are you now?"

"In West Sacramento."

"Okay, give me the address and I'll come right over."

"Maybe I should just drive over to your office." I moved away from the window and shut the curtains.

"That's not a good idea. "Your car's description and license are the bulls eye for every cop in town. They'd nail you before you crossed the Capitol Bridge. Let me call Lieutenant Thurber. She's the lead on this. I'll tell her you and I are coming in within the hour so you can give yourself up."

"Okay. If you think that's best." Everything was happening so fast, I didn't know if Mark's idea was smart or not. I gave Mark the IML address and awaited his arrival.

In my panic, I had a hard time getting my head around all of it. I thought more about the Krabbe e-mail and the missing Pam1111 ones. Why did the Krabbe e-mail remain and not the others? Her e-mail looked incriminating. The others did, too, so why had someone deleted those? Maybe because they concerned another death, one thirteen years ago, one someone didn't want investigated. Krabbe's message alluded that I'd done something to harm my wife, though not in so many words, with an insinuation that I'd threatened Krabbe to keep her mouth shut. Then I'd called her back and left a message. Unless that message remained on her machine, the police could construe that I'd talked to Krabbe briefly last night, and our conversation led her to come see me in the morning. We argued, and I shot her.

A thoroughly airtight set up. Removing the Pam1111 e-mails pointed to my unknown accuser as the one who'd set me up. I absolutely had to make our meeting the following night. I called Mark.

"If I turn myself in, how long before I make bail?"

"I don't know for sure. The DA will move for no bail. I'll counter at a half-million, but the going rate for murder is a million dollars. My guess will be three to four days before a judge will have time to review it and make a decision."

Three to four days. If I turned myself in, I'd miss the meeting with Pam1111.

"Thurber is all set for us," Mark continued. "She agreed there would be no media. I'm to call her when we're there and she'll meet us at a side entrance. It's a big favor."

"Tell her I'll turn myself in by midnight the day after tomorrow."

"Very funny, Ray."

"I'm serious. I've got to do something that might clear this whole thing up. If I'm in jail I won't be able—"

"Are you out of your mind!" Mark Scofield never raised his voice. He did now. "I already made the deal. If you renege now it makes me look bad. And your chances for bail will go out the window."

"I'm sorry, Mark," I said and hung up my phone. I turned off the ringer and stuck it in my pocket.

Another glance out the window confirmed that for now the police had no idea where to find me. I found a Swiss Army knife in a drawer in Rubia's desk. Two doors down, a swanky black Mercedes was parked in front of the massage parlor. Using the screwdriver tool on the knife I swapped my license plates for those on the Mercedes.

Once I pulled out of the IML parking lot, I was officially on the lam. When you're fifty-two years old with no criminal history, surviving on the street for a day and a half, while avoiding arrest, seemed a tall task. The police car that pulled behind me as I maneuvered onto Harbor Boulevard suggested that I might have just utterly failed.

twenty-six

I drove the posted speed limit west on Harbor, venturing an occasional glance in the rearview mirror at the cop. At the first stoplight, he moved from the right lane to the left and pulled even with my car at the limit line. He glanced over at me. I looked to my right, making a show of craning my neck as if something of extreme interest caught my attention inside the walls of the nearby Yummy Donuts.

Risking a glance back to the stoplight, then the cop, I caught him giving my car and me a once over. When the light turned green we both started forward. He continued on while I made a right at the corner, driving three more blocks before making another right turn and eventually working my way south on Jefferson Boulevard. I drove two miles, constantly checking my rearview mirror and glancing down side streets as I passed them, pulling into Southport Town Center, a shopping center with a Wells Fargo Bank. I hustled to the outdoor ATM, waving and smiling at the security camera, and was relieved to find that my account had not been locked. I withdrew four hundred dollars, my daily maximum, and hurried back to my car and drove off. That would be the last time I could use a debit or credit card for the next couple of days. As it was, the transaction no doubt had Thurber immediately directing every patrol car in the area to the bank.

I had to get my car—swapped out license plate or not— and myself out of sight as soon as possible. Think, think, think. Getting out of West Sacramento became priority number one. Returning to Sacramento seemed to be a bad idea as well. I continued south on

Jefferson, which bordered the Sacramento River Deep Water Channel, the delta pathway between the Pacific Ocean and the Port of West Sacramento. For thirty minutes I drove, my nerves easing only slightly, believing that the police would be focusing their search efforts where I'd last been seen. Oh, no. A sudden thought hit me. My cell phone. With a warrant, the police could track my whereabouts using my cell phone. I pulled to the side of the road, jumped out of my car, hopped a short barbed wire fence, and jogged to the end of the channel. Once I'd removed the battery, I tossed it and the phone into the water.

If the police had been tracking me, their hunt would soon turn to where I stood at that moment.

The delta afforded vast open spaces, and lots of nooks and crannies to hide in. It also offered just two main roads and only a handful of lodging options. With helicopters, they'd spot my car unless I ditched it in a garage or under some foliage, effectively stranding me at that spot. Damned if I kept going, damned if I turned around.

Just past Courtland I turned left on to Road 220 towards River Road, which I took north, crossing over to the east side of the river past Clarksburg, just beyond the spot of Pam's accident. Passing the Freeport Grill, I rejected my urge to stop and use the phone there; I'd have to get a hold of Rubia some other way. North on Freeport Boulevard, past Pocket Road, returned me to Sacramento. Before I reached Executive Airport, I turned left into the parking lot of the Gadsen Motel, a seedy-looking place that I'd driven past literally thousands of times and never given a thought. I parked my car behind a dumpster that shielded it from street view.

As I had hoped, the motel remained one of the few places in the world where you could rent a room for cash. I booked it for two nights, barely denting my bankroll. Upon entering the room, I could see the reason for the bargain price. The garish red and gold wallpaper blistered and frayed at its edges. A previous occupant had made a good attempt at removing it altogether, having peeled away enough to expose a huge chunk of untreated drywall. On the floor next to the sagging single bed was a short table lamp, somebody having absconded with the table on which it formerly stood. The only other furniture consisted of a plain wooden chair and a rickety desk. The carpet smelled of urine and cigarettes. My exploration of the bathroom ended after a quick glance. I hoped that a gas station, alley, or coffee can might avail itself before I would have to ever venture inside there. To my complete surprise, the phone on the floor next to the lamp produced a dial tone.

Darkness came a couple of hours later, providing enough cover for me to venture out. The minimart next door had sufficient supplies— toiletries, barely passable food, and bottled water—to get me through a couple of days.

After much internal debate, I decided to use the phone in my room to call the Say Hey, hoping that a judge would not have granted a tap of its phone since I didn't own the place or formally work there. The phone rang a dozen times before Rubia picked up.

"Ray, where are you? The cops have been here twice now. They want to arrest you for murder. They think I know where you are."

"I need a car. The police are looking for my mine. I changed the plates but they'll figure that out if they haven't already."

"I can get my cousin's car," she said after a pause. "He's out of town right now."

"Can you bring it over tonight?"

"I'm pretty sure the cops are watching. They'd follow me and I'd lead them to you. Let me call Cuellar and see if he can do it. It might not be until morning, though."

"That's okay." I gave her the address and room number to pass along to Cuellar.

"What are you going to do?" she said.

"I need to figure out what's going on. Someone set me up for killing a woman who used to work with my wife. They found her dead at my house. They must have put her body there, or killed her after I left this morning."

"You've really done it this time, professor."

"Tell me."

"Besides the car, can I do anything else to help?"

I thought about it for a moment. "There's one thing. I'm not sure when I'll be able to get to a computer. Do you have a pen?"

"Hold on."

When she returned I gave her the name of Susan Whitehead to see

128

if she could track down her obituary. More busy work than anything, but I knew Rubia wanted to feel that she was helping my cause. Besides, all day long I'd been grasping to figure out who could have set me up. Probably Pam1111. But who was that? I needed something, anything, to lead me to an answer to that question.

"Ray, be careful. The cops seem really pissed off. Even though you're a lame-assed white guy, and an old one at that, they'll shoot your ass in a heartbeat."

"Thanks for the delightful characterization, not to mention the sunny prediction. Have a nice day yourself."

"Seriously, Ray—"

"I know, Rubia. And thank you. Thank you for everything."

I hung up the phone and switched off the light. Sleep would be difficult, but at least the darkness spared a view of my dismal surroundings. I secured the deadbolt and went to the curtain to close the blackouts all the way, when I saw the motel manager who had checked me in. He was standing behind the dumpster looking closely at my car.

twenty-seven

After the manager returned from the dumpster to the office, I felt a little better when I noticed he was carrying an empty trash can. Before he entered his office, he glanced back at the dumpster. The light to the office went dark just after eleven, and a few seconds later another light switched on in the window next to the office, no doubt his living quarters. The light remained on as I watched through the curtains. Reading? Watching *The Tonight Show*? Calling the police and waiting for the fun to happen?

The phone in the room rang, causing me to jump. Might be the manager. Pondering that for a few seconds, I picked up after the fifth ring.

"Ray?"

"How did you get through to call?" I said to Rubia.

"You gave me the name and address of the motel. I called it and punched in your room number. You gave me that, too, remember."

"I guess I did. I'm a little antsy here. I'm surprised this fleabag has an automated phone system."

"Good news. I got a hold of Cuellar. He said he'd bring the car over to you. Good thing, too. Like I thought, there's a cop parked outside keeping an eye on me. Cuellar said he'd drop everything and do it as soon as he can."

"Thank you."

"Best thank him. He didn't even hesitate when I asked. Good guy.

130

Also, things slowed down at the bar a few minutes ago, so I looked up that Susan Whitehead obit for you. Took me awhile, she died a ways back."

"Thanks for doing that. Can you read it to me?" I said.

"Of course I can read it to you. I've got a college degree."

"Yeah, we let you slide on that, the degree thing. But I'll let you read it."

"Here goes. On a dark and stormy night—"

"It really starts like that?" I said.

"Of course not. Just seeing if you're paying attention. It is after your bedtime."

I walked the phone as far as the cord would allow me, which was to the foot of the bed. That enabled me to hold the receiver to my ear with my left hand, and to reach out with the fingertips of my right to part the curtains enough to view the manager's room. The light still shone through his window. The parking lot contained only five cars, which meant the vast majority of the rooms remained vacant. I wondered how the Gadsen Motel made enough money to have stayed in business for so long.

"'Susan Ann Whitehead passed away unexpectedly at the age of forty-seven on November 11,'" Rubia read. "'Born in Sacramento, she graduated from Rosemont High School, earned her Bachelors and Masters Degree in psychology from Sacramento State University and a PhD in psychology from UC Davis. She had her own clinical psychology practice in Carmichael for almost twenty years, where she helped patients young and old. She was a prolific writer and was published in a number of psychology trade journals. In addition to her work, Susan enjoyed taking long walks, reading, traveling, and spending time with family. She was preceded in death by her husband, US Army Sergeant James Whitehead, who served his country in Iraq. Susan is survived by daughter Angela C. Whitehead, sisters Melissa (James) Miller and Emily (Jack) Pearson, and brother, Herbert Hobson. Memorial Service will be held November 18 at St. John's Episcopal Church, Sacramento. In lieu of flowers, the family requests that donations be made to Al-Anon or to the Wounded Warrior Foundation.' That's the end of the obit, Ray."

"It doesn't say how she died?"

"That's all you got to say after I give the performance of my life reading that with such a flawless delivery?"

"I'd applaud but I'm holding the phone at the moment."

"No, it doesn't say how she died. I knew, nosey guy that you are, you would want to know that. So I looked through the online archives days before the obit ran. And guess what I found?"

"A news article about her death," I said.

"I don't know who's smarter, me or you."

"At the moment it would be you. You're the only one of us not wanted for murder and living in a rat-hole hotel managed by Norman Bates."

"Who's Norman Bates?"

"Don't tell me you've never seen the movie *Psycho*?"

"If it came out before *Pineapple Express* then it's not worth watching. Everything up till then wasn't any good."

"Our society's going to hell once your generation takes over. Now read the article."

"Wouldn't even call it an article. Just a little paragraph in the NewsLine section of the *Bee*. Here goes, 'A Sacramento woman was found dead in her Carmichael office last night by police officers checking on her when she did not return home at the end of her work day. The woman was identified as Susan Whitehead, 47, a licensed psychological therapist, who operated her own practice on the 4700 block of Manzanita Avenue. Captain Paul Smith, a spokesman for the Sacramento County Sheriff's Department, did not share details, calling the death "not suspicious." Non-suspicious deaths include those caused by accidents, suicide or natural causes. He said the body will be taken to the Sacramento County coroner's office to determine the cause of death.' That's all there is."

"That more or less aligns with what one of her former colleagues told me yesterday. He heard she drank herself to death."

"Doesn't drinking yourself to death usually mean, you know, over years? Like when you destroy you liver and stuff?"

"Not always," I said. "Not to be indelicate, but sometimes people drink too much and choke on their own vomit."

"Thanks a lot for that. Here I am in a bar, surrounded by alcohol, and you put that image in my head."

"It happens. Maybe she popped some pills along with the booze. At least the police thought it was accidental. And the obit mentions donating to Al-Anon."

"Can I ask who this woman is and why you care about her?" Rubia said.

"Probably nothing really. Pam may or may not have gone to a therapist the day she died, and this Whitehead was on the list is all."

"And that's important because …"

"I'm trying to find out what was on her mind. And maybe why she was driving around in the delta. But I guess I've struck out. She didn't see any of the other therapists from her company's EAP program. And this one is dead. Even so, all I have is Dana Krabbe's guess that she might have gone to see one. I'll probably never know if she actually did or not." I'd taken the psychologist angle as far as I could. "Wait a second. Read me the obit again."

"I knew you liked the way I read it." Rubia started to reread the obituary. Ray stopped her after the first sentence.

"She died on November 11, the same day as Pam. The same year. That's a coincidence."

"Yeah, and you know what they say."

"There's no such thing as coincidence."

The deaths on the same day set off rockets of possibility in my head. Finally, something had come together, though I had no idea what it meant. Both deaths happened so long ago that the odds of finding a connection, if any, between them were remote. "Can you read me the names of the family again?" Turning away from the window, I found a pen and stained pad of paper in the drawer of the desk. I wrote down the names as Rubia read.

"Anything else I can do for you, boss?"

"Maybe. You're in that LinkedIn social network thing, aren't you?"

"Yeah, regular mainstream chick."

"Can you log in to that?"

"Sure."

"You have no idea how helpless being off the grid makes you feel," I said.

"Yeah, you're a regular Henry David Walden. Back to nature and all that shit."

"His last name is Thoreau. And *Walden* was the book's title."

"Whatever."

"Besides, I doubt Walden Pond was populated with hookers and Johns," I said, moving back to the window and watching a couple of prostitutes and their customers walk from the street towards rooms at the motel. Now I knew how the motel made its money. Who needed a sophisticated business plan, or even clean rooms, when you had the world's oldest profession providing your cash flow?

"Okay, I'm in. What do you want from LinkedIn?"

"Can you find a Jason Upland and Ron or Ronald Patel?"

"Who are they?"

"A couple of guys who worked with my wife at Crazy Zebra Enterprises."

"Your wife worked at Crazy Zebra? They're big time."

"Yeah, she did. Head of the finance department." Where they worked her ragged.

"Wow, smart chick. Wonder what she saw in you?"

"Eye candy."

"Must suck being nothing more than a fashion accessory for women," she said.

"My cross to bear. Any luck with LinkedIn?"

"Don't be so touchy. Why do you want me to look into them?"

"I don't know," I said. "I'm just getting the feeling this all relates, somehow, to Crazy Zebra."

"Why?"

"No real reason. Maybe it was what Dana Krabbe told me. Or maybe it's because nothing else seems to be in play other than her work."

"Here we go," Rubia said. "There are three Jason Uplands. One's still in college, so I'm guessing you don't care about him."

"What about the other two? Are either of them in California or on the West Coast?"

"Yeah, this guy here is. Jason Upland is the CFO for a company called Liberty Global Investments in Walnut Creek, corner of Treat and Bancroft. Been there seven years. He's married with two kids. No other contact or personal information."

"That's okay," I said, jotting down the company name and location. "What about Patel?"

"Hold on. Let's see here ... okay, here we go. There's a Ron Patel, also in the Bay Area, at a company called Megadata Dynamics. He is a management analyst who has worked there for five years. MBA from Sac State. Looks like their office is in San Mateo, on Third Avenue, just off El Camino. You want his e-mail address?"

"No, that's okay. I think it's better that I talk with him in person."

"Anything else you want?"

I thought for a second. "Demetrio's family has probably heard that the police want to arrest me for murder. Could you call and reassure them?"

"Already done."

"And Sara?"

"Yep. She said to tell you she loves you."

I thanked Rubia and hung up the phone. In the parking lot, another hooker escorted a customer into a room. The motel manager's light remained on. I maintained a vigil at the window until two in the morning, finally deciding to give sleep a try once I saw his light go out and the fatigue began to overtake me. I took off my shoes and lay on top of the bed, using my coat as a blanket, not wanting to climb under the sheets of the soiled bed.

My eyes started to close under their own weight when headlights pierced the narrow gap between the blackout drapes. The lights went black, followed by several seconds of silence.

A moment later, someone knocked loudly on my door.

twenty-eight

I jumped out of bed. Carefully, I parted the drapes to see a dark sedan parked in front of my room. A dark Ford with no markings. Didn't cops drive Fords? In vain, I tried to see who stood at my door. I looked through the peephole, but it was too grimy to be of use.

The knocks came again.

I slid over to the side of the door. "Who is it?"

"Ray, it's me, Cuellar."

I exhaled in relief and let him in. He moved quickly inside and I turned on the overhead light. In his arms he carried a brown grocery bag.

"I didn't expect you until later this morning," I said.

"Rubia told me how important it was, so I thought it best to get here as soon as I could. It took me awhile to pick up the car and find someone who could drive me back."

"I can't thank you enough."

"Don't mention it. Can I put this on the desk?" He set the bag down and pulled out a bottle of Hoppy's IPA and a cardboard food container. He handed the container to me. "I thought you might be hungry so I got you a cheeseburger and fries from Suzie Burger. Thought you could use a beer, too. Do you have an opener?"

"You're awesome," I said, pulling out the Swiss Army knife and handing it to him.

He opened the beer as I sat on the edge of the bed to start in on the burger. "Aren't you going to join me?" I said.

"Not hungry, but I brought a couple of beers." He opened a second beer and sat in the chair at the desk. His eyes roamed the room as he took in the bleak quarters.

"Nice place, huh?" I said.

"To say the least."

We both sipped our beers and I started in on the burger, the first bite reminding me of my suppressed hunger. "I appreciate you doing this," I said between bites. "You hardly know me, so it's above and beyond. Thanks."

He nodded and took another sip of beer. "I won't ask what your trouble is, but if there's anything else I can do to help, just let me know."

I thought about telling him the whole story, but settled for a shortened version instead. "The police want me for something that I didn't do. I need to buy a couple of days to prove them wrong."

He nodded, not judging, just taking it in.

"Rubia really is very impressed with your work so far," I said. "Wishes she could hire you full-time."

"Her work is important. I'm grateful for whatever hours she can give me."

I finished the burger and about half of the french fries, washing it all down with the rest of my beer. Cuellar had only drunk about half his when he stood to leave.

"My ride is parked out on the street waiting for me. I should probably go now."

I thanked him again and he left. A couple of minutes later, I picked up the keys he left on the desk and got inside the car, a Chevy Impala, not a Ford after all. I didn't want the nosey manager to see it when he awoke in the morning, and poke around it as well. I pulled onto Freeport, turning right at the next street and pulling over after just a few feet. There were no "No Parking" signs, so I left the car there and started walking back, the couple of hundred yards to the motel.

A man strode briskly from the motel parking lot to a car parked on Freeport. He looked up and down the street, then back at the motel, before ducking into his car and driving away, tires squealing. One of the Johns leaving his tryst. I reached the parking lot and started for my room. The aroma of cigarette smoke wafted through the cool fall air. One of the prostitutes sat on a chair outside her room, its door still open.

"Hey, there," she said to me. "Looking for a date?"

"No thanks." I said, continuing to walk on.

"Forty bucks."

"Thanks, anyway."

"You're really missing out," she called out as I reached my door and entered my room.

This motel, just five miles from my house, existed in an entirely different world than mine. I wondered what other activities occurred behind these dreary walls—drug sales, drug use, all forms of consensual and non-consensual sex, nothing seemed to be too tawdry to stage here—all leaving behind a stink and a grime that nothing short of burning down the motel could eliminate. God, I wanted to get out of there. It was only three in the morning, too early to accomplish anything. Against my better judgment I used the bathroom to brush my teeth. I shaved and splashed water on my face. One look into the shower stall banished any notion of using it.

With no television or radio to pass the time, I paced the room. By three-thirty, I couldn't take another second inside, so I went back out into the early morning, hoping that a short walk and the fresh air would lift my spirits. I made it to the sidewalk without encountering a hooker or a John when the squawking of a radio caught my attention. Six police cars lined Freeport to my left, with maybe a dozen cops, donned in bulletproof vests and helmets, huddled on the sidewalk.

They came to bust the prostitutes, I rationalized at first. No, if they came for the prostitutes they would have done so hours ago, when they were out walking the street and luring customers. And I doubted busting hookers required bulletproof vests and helmets. I walked back from the sidewalk towards my room. The light in the motel manager's room was on again. Damn him! I had to get out of there. Freeport Boulevard was out of the question. On that well-lit street, at least one of the cops would spot me, the only person out walking at such an hour. I jogged the remaining distance to my room, locked it, then gathered up my wallet and car keys.

The manager had no doubt told them where I'd stashed my car and reported my room number. I had to get out of there, so I dashed to the only other spot I could think of that would be safe, at least for a few minutes.

"What do you want?" the hooker said behind her closed door.

"I changed my mind," I said. "We talked a couple of minutes ago."

"Go away. I'm sleeping."

"I've got a hundred bucks."

"Go away!"

Glancing over my shoulder I saw the first of the police cars pulling into the motel parking lot, not a hundred feet from where I stood.

"Two hundred."

The latch rattled on the other side of the door, which she opened a crack to peek at me.

"Oh, it's you," said the prostitute who'd propositioned me a few minutes before. "Come on in."

Inside, I went to her window to see if the police had seen me. All six cars had parked in the middle of the lot, two nose-to-nose, blocking the entrance. Two cops, weapons drawn, crouched behind the hood of each car. Another two cops headed for my car, and three went around to the back of the building. Five started towards the front door of the room I had just vacated.

"Where's the two hundred bucks?" the woman said.

My hands shaking, I extracted at least ten twenties and thrust them at her. She shuffled through the bills, nodded, and tossed them onto the desk.

"Take your clothes off," she said.

But I was already heading to the bathroom, carrying a table lamp. At the small window, I used the bottom of the lamp to break out the glass. It was loud but I figured the police had radios in their ears and their attention fixed on my room.

"Hey, what the hell are you doing? That's gonna cost you extra."

The bathroom window was over the shower stall and measured maybe three feet wide and a foot and a half tall. I brought over the desk chair and set it in front of the window, and began to pull myself up to the window, cutting both my hands on broken glass in the process. Using my legs to push myself up from the chair, I finally got my head through the opening and my waist up to the window's ledge.

"Raymond Courage, this is the police," commanded a deep-voiced cop on a loudspeaker. "Open the door slowly and walk out of the room with your hands up."

I dropped through the window to the dirt below. The room I had rented was around the corner of the L-shaped building, so the three police dispatched to the back of my room could not see me. At least not yet. A narrow strip of dirt separated the motel from a sagging wooden fence. I climbed up and over the fence, landing in dense shrubbery that poked through my shirt and pants. It took a few seconds to extricate myself and get my bearings. I stood in the back yard of a humble house, the darkness offering little more information than that. Until I heard the growling. Before I could see it, a dog had its teeth firmly embedded in my calf. I swatted at it, resisting the urge to yell or scream.

Once again a policeman commanded that I give myself up.

It would not be much longer before they burst into the room and find it empty. The dog growled and tried to reset its grip on my calf, which I used as an opening to pull my leg away and swat the dog again on the snout. It was a small dog, maybe fifteen pounds, with enough attitude for a pack of pit bulls. The thing lunged at me, this time aiming at my crotch. I caught it mid-leap, holding it at arm's length as it wriggled ferociously, trying to break free. I carried the dog across the yard to a gate at the side of the house. A padlock dangled from the hasp, locking closed the six-foot-high gate.

From the motel, two loud shots rang out followed by breaking glass. They had no doubt fired tear gas into my room. In less than a minute, they'd storm inside. I tossed the dog as far as I could. It landed with a yelp, recovered quickly, and charged me again. Its teeth clamped down on my pant leg as I pulled myself onto the gate, the weight of the dog hampering my ascent. I managed to get my left leg over the top of the gate, but the dog held fast to my pant leg, dangling a couple of feet off the ground. I shook my leg and heard my pants rip as the dog tumbled to the ground.

Just as I landed on the other side of the gate, lights came on inside the house. The dog barked angrily at the gate. I ran towards the street, and the car parked a couple of hundred feet away, when I heard a door bang open.

"Hey you, stop!" someone yelled, just as I reached the Chevy.

A man raced towards me from the house. I fumbled with the key fob to open the door.

"I've got a gun," the man called out. *"Stop!"*

A gunshot—loud and not from the hotel—exploded in the darkness. He held the gun straight up. It had been a warning shot.

"Next one's at you. I'm tired of you punks stealing my shit." He walked purposefully towards me, the gun steadied in his hand.

Finally, I managed to open the door and start the car. He grabbed the handle of the car as I threw it into gear. Another gunshot, this one shattering the left rear window, deafened me.

The ringing in my ears did not stop until I passed through Stockton, some forty miles away.

November 16

twenty-nine

"You are too good to me," said Mina Stawkowski, as she lay naked under the sheets in Yuri Mastrov's bed. She had just opened the gift box containing a pair of three-carat diamond earrings.

Mastrov shrugged as he toweled himself dry after his morning shower. Of all his mistresses, he liked Mina the best. She knew the rules and followed them. She didn't whine like some of the others. Or worse, call and ask to see him. Mina knew that Mastrov did the calling. You did not ask about his wife. You did not ask about his daughter. You did not ask about his business. When he called, you came. If you followed the rules you were rewarded with great sex, luxurious trips, and fabulous gifts.

"Once you have showered you can leave," he told her, pulling on a pair of gray wool trousers.

"You don't want me to stay tonight?" Her voice held a hint of disappointment.

"No." Mastrov's wife would be returning later that evening by private jet after her monthly shopping excursion to Paris. She knew of her husband's dalliances. Her rules were not dissimilar from Mina's and the others—do not ask about the other women. The reward for following that simple rule was a lifestyle few women could dream about. "I'll have a driver pick you up in an hour."

Mina did not need to be told to avoid the main section of the sixteen-thousand-square-foot home. She already knew that other inviolable rule of staying out of sight from Mastrov's daughter.

142

Mastrov cinched up his tie and shifted his shoulders to set his suit jacket so it felt just right. He confirmed in the mirror what he already knew. He looked damn good.

"Good bye, Yuri," he heard her say as he left the bedroom. He didn't respond.

He walked through the house and out into the spacious grounds of his Granite Bay mansion. He'd bought it twelve years ago for eleven million, a bargain in his mind. If the home had been located in Beverly Hills or Bel Air it would easily cost three or four times that amount.

He proceeded down the marble path in the backyard, rows of palm trees on either side, admiring the spectacular view of the rolling green foothills and Folsom Lake. Past the two par-three golf holes and three outdoor tennis courts, he came to the property's most recent addition, the indoor tennis facility. Even before he opened the door he could hear the satisfying *thwack* of racket on ball and it made him smile. The indoor court's temperature had been set to a perfect seventy degrees, just as his daughter liked it.

He sat at a round patio table, where a pitcher of fresh-squeezed orange juice, carafe of coffee, fresh fruit, and a platter of croissants and pastries had been set. On the court, Elena Mastrov hit with her personal tennis pro, a man Yuri had lured away from Arden Hills Tennis Club two years ago, by offering a hefty raise and a new Porsche.

He loved watching his daughter hit, her groundstrokes flawless, athletic movements of beauty, grace and, above all, power. The world would be hers for the taking one day. Beautiful, athletic, smart, and with all the resources he could afford, at her disposal. He poured himself a glass of orange juice and sat back to watch the practice session continue.

Root entered a few minutes later, taking a seat at the table, Mastrov barely glancing at him. They sat silently and watched Elena and the pro play, the girl finally winning a long point with an overhead volley.

"She's good," Root said.

"Number four in Northern California," Mastrov said, not with pride but a tinge of disappointment. With all the money spent on private lessons, personal trainers and coaches, tournaments around the world, and the best equipment, he'd hoped by now she might be number one, not in Northern California, but in the country. That's what Mastrovs did, ascended to the top. One day, maybe she will. "Have some coffee, Daniel," he added, preferring his employee's given name to his nickname. The sex with Mina, her reaction to his gift, and now watching his beautiful daughter's elegant play elevated him, putting him in an unusually expansive mood.

Root poured himself a cup of coffee and took a testing sip.

"She'll be playing in college next year," Mastrov said. "The Harvard coach has offered her a spot on the roster for next year, as long as the admissions office accepts her application." The coach had said that with a wink, knowing that a word from her, coupled with Elena's perfect grades and SAT scores, made her a shoo-in for admission.

Wordlessly, the two men watched the pair play two more points, Elena taking the first one, the pro the second.

"A big night tonight," Mastrov said.

"Yes."

"Are you confident in your plan?"

"Yes."

"Do you have the manpower you need to succeed?"

"Absolutely."

Despite having instructed Lobo to give his number two security man more responsibility, Mastrov felt a bit apprehensive. He didn't know any details, just that Root would run the operation, Lobo sitting it out. This man had all the smarts it took, and the same detached ruthlessness as Lobo, traits that made them thorough in every detail, from set up to execution to clean up.

When he'd considered hiring Daniel "The Root of All Evil" Bennington many years before, Mastrov at first had doubts, thinking the former fighter might be too impulsive. Fourteen years later, he was glad he'd ignored his doubts about the man. Daniel's value to Crazy Zebra and Mastrov had been proven many times. "When you are successful this entire problem will be resolved?"

"I guarantee it. It was a loose end that came out of nowhere. Probably not a big deal but to be sure, we'll squash it."

"That's what I want to hear," Mastrov said. "You can go."

144

Root departed. His boss stayed and watched his daughter play on. What a great morning it'd been so far, he thought to himself. What a great morning to be a billionaire.

thirty

At six in the morning, Bay Area rush hour traffic began to build until a solid stream of headlights moved in both directions on I-680. Southbound cars started to back up at the Highway 242 split as I pulled off in Walnut Creek, at the Treat Boulevard, and proceeded a few blocks to where it intersected Bancroft. A sign reading "Liberty Global Investments" marked the spot where Jason Upland worked.

He probably wouldn't arrive at the office for a couple of hours, and my current condition would not inspire a receptionist to allow access to a chief financial officer. Continuing down Treat for a couple of miles, I eventually came upon a small shopping center anchored by a CVS Pharmacy. I parked in a corner of the lot and removed the chunks of glass remaining in my rear side window. I found a towel in the trunk, which I used to sweep out most of the glass from the back seat. At least now the car didn't look like a mobile crime scene.

The same could not be said about me. In the early light just after sunrise, I surveyed myself. The bleeding from my cut hands had stopped. I continued to extract thorns from my back, arms and legs, a painful process that had occupied me during the ninety-minute drive from Sacramento. Somewhere during my motel escape, I'd managed to scrape my face, and a nice set of doggie teeth marks decorated my right calf. Worse than my body's condition was that of my clothing, my pants shredded and stained courtesy of the dog and my adventures with window ledge, bushes, and fences. My shirt looked only slightly better.

Heads turned when I walked into CVS. Who could blame them? If

I saw me walking into a store, I would put as many aisles between us as possible. The good news: I was able to move up the line as everybody in front of me simultaneously remembered an item they had forgotten from a distant store shelf.

I emerged from the store with a first aid kit, pair of khaki pants, a long-sleeved red polo, and a bottle of water. Inside my car, I attended to my myriad wounds and changed into my new clothes. A few minutes later, I deemed myself ready for a public appearance, so I walked across the parking lot to a Panera Bread restaurant. I ordered a muffin and drank a cup of black coffee, confident that my identity remained anonymous here, where most people gleaned their news from San Francisco stations and websites, not those of Sacramento. To further confirm this, I leafed through a copy of the morning's *San Francisco Chronicle* that an earlier patron had left in a basket at the restaurant's entrance, finding nothing about Dana Krabbe or me. The Bay Area had its own issues to deal with, without the need to add Sacramento crimes into the mix.

An hour later, resplendent in my new thirty-dollar-wardrobe, I sat opposite Jason Upland in his firm's lobby in a chrome and black leather chair, straight out of *The Jetsons*. He was good-looking, right around forty, with a full head of dark hair and a stylish beard.

"Are you okay?" he said, referring to the scrape on my cheek.

"Fine. Golfing accident."

He chewed on that a moment before deciding not to follow up.

"You said you had questions about my time at Crazy Zebra when I worked with your wife. What did you want to know?"

"Do you recall when she died?"

"In the car accident? Of course, it was horrible. And I'm sorry by the way. I know it's been awhile but I'm sure it still must hurt."

"Thank you," I said, pausing before continuing. "Was my wife unusually stressed on the day she died?"

He thought for a moment as he stroked that stylish beard. I had the suspicion that he did that a lot. "You know, now that I think about it, I wasn't even in the office that day. I was back in New York working with the bankers helping us set up our IPO. But everyone in our office was stressed during that time. We were going from a privately held firm to a big public company. It was the biggest IPO in Sacramento, and one of the biggest ever in the country."

"Yeah, she was stressed for months," I said. "I'm sure everyone else was, too. Did her death set back the IPO? I don't remember. Once she died, I didn't pay much attention."

"Not really. They hired some guy from Wall Street to take over. Plus, Ron and I were already neck-deep into it, so we kind of kept things going until the new guy came on board."

"How come they didn't promote you to take the position, since you were already 'neck-deep' as you said.?"

"No," he said. "Ron and I were only a couple of years out of business school. We weren't ready for that. And, frankly, even if they had offered it to me, I'd have turned them down. It would have been too much for me at the time."

"Do you remember the name of the person who came in to replace my wife?"

He stroked his beard some more. "Westbrook or Westmore. Something like that. I don't remember exactly. He left just over a year later, right before I did."

"Why would you both leave so soon after the IPO was issued? Seems like it would be a great experience for your careers. And lucrative, too."

"I can't speak for him, but for me it was a tough place to work. Even after the IPO, there was so much work to be done with ridiculous deadlines. I took the money I made with my stock holdings on the IPO and left."

"So you were looking for something less stressful." I said.

"That was part of it. The culture there was a little different."

"How so?"

"Well, let's just say Mr. Mastrov liked to play a little fast and loose. A little too much so for my taste. I'm not saying he ever did anything illegal, but some of our accounting practices weren't done the way I was taught in business school. I'll just leave it at that."

Five minutes later, Upland headed off to a meeting, while I returned to my car for a trip across San Francisco Bay, taking the Dumbarton Bridge under a sky of high clouds. Out on the bay, a couple of dozen sailboats took advantage of the wind blowing in from the Pacific.

I arrived at Ron Patel's San Mateo office building by ten-thirty. Though the name Megadata Dynamics suggested a formidable corporate presence, the company's office was quite modest, maybe big enough for fifty employees. I waited in the simple lobby, leafing through old editions of *Men's Health* and *Outside*. By noon, he had yet to appear, the elderly receptionist apologizing three times for his tardiness. When he did arrive, just after the top of the hour, he informed me he had less than five minutes to spare.

"My running group leaves in a couple of minutes," he said, which explained his attire of shorts, singlet, and high tech running shoes. "We're training for the California International Marathon."

I refrained from making a smart remark; I had, after all, come unexpectedly. He didn't owe me any of his time. "I can walk with you to where you need to be if that would help," I said.

We walked out the front of the building. During my hour and a half waiting in the lobby, the early morning clouds had drifted away, rendering a bright blue sky and a flawless fall afternoon. I half felt like running with him.

"My secretary said you wanted to talk about Crazy Zebra."

"Yes, my wife worked there."

"Pam?"

I nodded.

"Sorry, I didn't put your last name with hers. Ray Courage. I'm so sorry for your loss. What a terrible thing that was?"

I nodded. "Did you happen to see or talk with Pam that day, the day of the accident?"

"I'm trying to think." He stopped on the sidewalk in front of his building and began to stretch, pulling his right foot up until it touched the seat of his shorts. "She was in meetings pretty much all day, every day, leading up to the IPO. I remember that. But I do remember seeing her that day because she looked upset. Pam usually was pretty easy-going. Not much ruffled her feathers, even in those stressful times."

"Did she say anything about why she was so upset?"

"Not exactly. Well, maybe a little." He changed feet, now easing

149

his left foot up to stretch his quadriceps. "We were trying to get the IPO prospectus report out the next week. That was a big deal, and a lot of pressure on all of us, but especially on her. Something about it wasn't right, so much so that she said she couldn't sign off on it."

"Why would she say that?" I felt a bit embarrassed that I didn't know much about my wife's work at Crazy Zebra. Maybe if I had, I could have been more comfort to her. And that line of logic could take me a long ways—to Pam not dying, to my not being wanted for killing Dana Krabbe.

Patel looked around nervously. "I was really young then, mid-twenties. I didn't know how things worked. I figured you just did what the big boss says and everything would be cool. Pam couldn't do that."

"What exactly couldn't she do?"

"I wasn't in all the meetings and didn't have any real information. I mean, that was a long time ago. I don't remember all the details, but … but there was talk in the finance office that Crazy Zebra's cash position was not as good as it claimed in the prospectus. Some money, like a half-billion dollars' worth, was going to be wired into our account to justify that we were worth investing in. Then we were going to send it back with a generous interest payment after the IPO. That was the rumor, anyway. Pam never said so, but I think that's why she wouldn't sign off on it."

"So it was like a loan?"

"That's how I looked at it. But your wife didn't. I think she believed it would be deceptive at best, illegal at worst. So she wouldn't sign off on the prospectus."

"Who was going to lend the money?"

"Not sure. Again, it was all rumor. I heard that it was coming from some of Mastrov's contacts in Russia. Black market stuff. But who knows?"

"When the IPO went public, was that wad of cash in the Crazy Zebra account?"

"Yeah."

At the street corner, a group of four runners bounced up and down on their toes, loosening up, waiting for the traffic light to change.

"That's really all I know," Patel said. Before I could say thank you or ask another question, he started running towards the other runners as the light turned green.

So much more needed doing before my meeting with Pam1111 tomorrow evening. Without a phone, Internet access, or the freedom to travel the streets of Sacramento unmolested by the police, I decided to stay in the safer environs of the Bay Area a little longer.

Just up the street from Patel's office, I found the San Mateo Public Library. I spent the first half-hour on the Internet learning as much as I could about Yuri Mastrov and Crazy Zebra Enterprises, learning very little more than I already knew. His sports television network did much better than I would have guessed, whetting the nation's appetite for mixed martial arts, cage fighting, and other forms of brutal human combat.

I met the man exactly once, at Crazy Zebra's company picnic. He wore an expensive suit to the catered outdoor affair at his country club, while everyone else sported shorts or swimwear. Pam introduced him to me and we spoke for maybe thirty seconds, his interest in me waning when he learned I taught at Sacramento State, a calling of little value to a man like him. He seemed an arrogant prick and I took an immediate dislike to him, though I held my tongue so Pam would feel no need to defend him.

I do have to say that my feelings for him improved over the way he handled Pam's death. Not only did he offer to pay for Sara's later college costs, he kicked in an extra one hundred thousand dollars that he said would have been Pam's share of the IPO. Even when I found out later that her share would have been ten times this amount, I didn't hold any ill will towards him. He had been generous enough when he had no obligation to do so. I wondered now if his generosity was nothing more than an effort to placate me.

Exhausting the public information about Mastrov and his company, I turned to locating Susan Whitehead's surviving relatives. I found nothing on daughter Angela C. Whitehead, but for her sisters and brothers, I was able to find home phone numbers.

The librarian hesitated when I asked if I could use the office phone. She relented when I told her the calls were local, to a couple of friends I was worried about because they were late for our meeting at the library

Herbert Hobson hung up immediately after I asked him if he was Susan Whitehead's brother. I tried calling him three more times and he did not answer. The Sacramento number I found online for Emily Pearson turned out to be for her husband's cell phone. Since my name was in the local news, I just identified myself as an insurance investigator reopening the Susan Whitehead life insurance claim, and that it was likely the family might be receiving more money. He paused on the other end of the line for a few seconds before telling me to go screw myself.

Susan's sister, Melissa, answered the phone on the first ring.

This time I identified myself as a private investigator and asked if she was Susan's sister.

"What's this about?"

"I just had some questions about your sister."

"What kind of questions?"

"Just some general ones."

"This isn't about what happened back then, is it? My husband's dead. Can't you just leave it alone?"

"This is not about your husband. It's about—"

"Look, I'm late for an appointment." She hung up without another word.

Her paranoid tone piqued my interest. When I returned to Sacramento I would need to pay her a visit.

On my way out of the library, I put a twenty dollar bill in the "Support Your Library" box out of guilt for the long-distance calls. That left me about eighty bucks, enough to rent another room in a flophouse, where I hoped for a better night's sleep. Tomorrow promised to be a day of either elation or heartbreak, and I wished with all my heart that it would reunite me with the love of my life.

November 17

thirty-one

"Who is it?" came the timid female voice on the other side of the door.

"Ray Courage," I said, deciding to use my real name because Melissa Miller struck me as someone who might ask for my identification. I had to chance that she'd not read or heard my name on the news. "We spoke yesterday. I called about your sister Susan."

Melissa said nothing. I stood on the porch of her small bungalow. The east Sacramento neighborhood had long served as a haven to well-educated professionals desiring proximity to downtown's workplaces and nightlife. Most homes in the neighborhood had been renovated with attention to detail. This was not the case for Miller's home. The craftsman style home badly needed the attention of a craftsman, its green paint peeling, the wooden porch rotting, and several porch railings snapped and broken.

Standing there darkened my mood, which had already become gloomy during the drive back from the Bay Area. Until the past few months, my life had been one of mundane routine that I loved and appreciated. Work by day as a college professor, raising a daughter and sending her to college, living in a safe and normal neighborhood—stuff of the American Dream. Now here I stood, a fugitive, badgering strangers for insights into how I might escape my current condition as Public Enemy Number One. The human brain has a hard time processing such a shift in reality. Trust me on this.

"I have nothing to say about her," she said at last.

"Please, it will only take a second. It could be very important."

"What agency are you with?"

"I'm not with an agency or anything like that. I need to find out whether my wife saw your sister professionally years ago."

No sound came from the other side of the door for nearly a minute, convincing me that she had retreated, stranding me on her porch until I grew bored and departed. I began to knock again when I heard two solid clicks of dead bolts opening. She opened the door warily, enough for one eye to peek out at me.

"Who is your wife?"

"Pamela Courage. She might have seen your sister the day before she died. I'm trying to see if she did."

"I wouldn't have any idea. My sister and I didn't talk much, and we didn't talk about her work at all. She was this fancy doctor. And I was just a housewife. Our lives took different paths. Except for holidays now and again, we hardly saw each other."

"You never heard my wife's name mentioned?" I said, knowing the answer but needing to confirm it.

"No. Like I said, if she was a patient, I wouldn't have had any idea. Now, I have to go."

"One quick question," I said before she could shut the door on me.

She waited, peering at me through that sliver of an opening. In that one eye I saw fear and distrust, something you might see in a beaten animal. A hunch told me that this woman lived in a perpetual state of anxiety, suspicious of anyone who said as much as hello.

"I'm trying to find Susan's daughter Angela. Do you know where she lives now?"

She looked down to the floor with that single eye before parting the door enough so that I could see her face in full. She had the pale, puffy face of someone who seldom ventured outdoors, a middle-aged woman who long ago had the human feelings of hope, desire, and confidence ripped from her soul.

"That was a long time ago," she said, the same words she had said yesterday on the phone.

"What was a long time ago? When Susan died?"

"We never wanted kids, Jim and me. I mean, I did, but I knew we

154

couldn't. Not the way he was."

I didn't know what she was talking about, though I could also see that I had launched her into a contemplative state, her eyes growing distant to another place and time. She mumbled something to herself.

"At first I said no, we didn't want the girl. My cheapskate brother and my selfish sister refused to take her. Social Services said that they were going to have to put her in a foster home until someone adopted her. She was odd, even back then. No one would adopt her. She'd spend the next ten years moving from foster home to foster home."

"This is Angela we're talking about?"

"My sister and I weren't close, like I said. But I couldn't let her child be put into the system. I told myself I could protect her, keep her safe. Then there was the trust fund money. I'm not proud of it but that played a part. My sister's will gave us enough money to raise her and then some. That's what made us take her in."

If Angela had been eight years old at the time of her mom's death, she would be of no use to me. It was highly doubtful her mom would talk to an eight-year-old about her patients, especially one she saw exactly once, if at all.

"At first, we all got along good," Melissa continued, as if I wasn't there. "Then she got older. Around twelve, thirteen, she got those little titties. I think it started happening around when she turned fourteen."

"What are you talking about?" I said. My skin felt tighter, and instinctively I crossed my arms across my chest.

"The little bitch loved the attention. She knew she had become the center of attention in our house. She never liked me from the get-go. And now she had it all over me."

"I don't know what you're talking about." Though in a way I did, growing more uncomfortable by the second.

"It had probably gone on for months, maybe even a year or more. Then I caught them. Came home early from the store 'cause I forgot my grocery list. I won't even tell you what they were doing. Sick. I knew the bastard always had a thing for the little girls. The way he talked about 'em. But his own niece? And she looked like she liked it. Bitch."

The child abuse horrified me. I couldn't find anything to say.

"I finally reported him when she turned sixteen," she continued. "Like I said, she was always strange. Cutting herself, throwing up her food. When she tried to kill herself, I knew I needed to turn him in. Turn in my Jim. The CPS investigators came but she wouldn't tell on him, so nothing happened. I used that trust fund money and sent her away to a boarding school down in Monterey. I even used some of the money to get her therapy. A lot of good that did.

She started to cry, softly, the tears streaming down her cheeks. She looked away, at something inside the house out of my sight.

"I'm sorry if I brought back bad memories," I said.

"A year later, when she came home for the first time on school break, she killed him."

"Oh, my god."

"They never proved it, of course. But she was out driving. Knew he went out jogging. Knew the route he ran. She came back to the house about the time I heard the sirens. Bitch killed him. That's what you should be investigating. She murdered him!"

Her crying deepened, her chest heaving, trying to endure the immense sorrow. I didn't want to leave her like that, and yet I didn't see how I could console her standing outside her door. I felt sorry for her. I also felt anger, that she had let such things happen in her home. Who could blame a teenager wanting to harm the man who had attacked and abused her for years? Melissa Miller owned the responsibility to protect that child and she'd failed. Worse than fail, she had enabled her husband's sick perversion. Part of me wanted to tell her so, but that would be piling on this wretched woman, whose life had become its own punishment, a lonely existence filled with horrible memories, misguided hatred, and no hope. I turned to leave.

"You find her! You find Claire and put her in jail!"

"Claire? I thought her name was Angela?"

Melissa shook her head violently. "No, sir, we changed her last name to ours when we legally adopted her. Then she wanted to start going by her middle name. Said she liked it better'n Angela. So that's what we did. Started calling her Claire. Claire Miller."

thirty-two

The Sacramento weather was unusually warm, bright, and cheery, a stark contrast to Carla Thurber's mood. She sat in her unmarked Sac PD car in front of Ray Courage's house on the remote chance he might return. Her impatience growing by the minute, she reached for her cell phone and called Mark Scofield, her fifth call to him in the last twenty-four hours.

"Well?" she said, skipping the formalities when the lawyer picked up.

"Still no word."

"What are you doing about that?" she said tersely.

"Same thing I told you the last time you called, which according to my watch was a little over an hour ago, and that's nothing. I have no idea where he went. Maybe if you guys hadn't spooked him the other night at the motel, and sent him running, he would have turned himself in by now."

"Fat chance of that. And we're adding resisting arrest, failure to obey a police officer, and whatever else I can think of. We're going to charge him for the cost of the motel operation on top of that."

"You can't do that."

"Watch me." Thurber didn't like the fact she couldn't rattle Scofield. Maybe he didn't know where his client was, but she expected him to make some effort, anything, to find him.

"Believe me, he'll come in when he's ready. All I ask is that you and Sac PD show restraint when he does. He doesn't carry a gun,

157

doesn't believe in them. He's no threat to the police or anyone else. So please respect his rights."

"You're in no position to dictate terms of his arrest. And for you to imply that we would unnecessarily harm your client is an insult."

"We're done here," Scofield said and hung up the phone.

Damn. She had planned to hang up on him and he beat her to it. One small little victory and he denied her even that. Yesterday this case had her practically skipping down the halls of homicide division. In a day her ascending star had made a U-turn, hurtling back at her with career-ruining force. Ray Courage. Son of a bitch. How had a middle-aged college professor managed to get away from her? How had he fooled them thirteen years ago?

She went through the evidence in her head one more time. Courage had gone to Dana Krabbe's house the day before the murder, ostensibly to intimidate her to keep her mouth shut about something. There was the note he'd left with her address written on it in what looked like his handwriting and with his fingerprints on it. The smashed beer bottle, also with his prints, proved he was there and likely pissed off. No coincidence that Krabbe worked with the man's wife, dead wife, when she was killed. Next, Krabbe's e-mail to Courage implying he was coercing her to keep quiet, followed up by his phone call to her. Krabbe's visit the next day, either because he invited her with the phone call or something he had said prompted her to see him. Either way she ended up at his house, shot in his living room. Throw in the fact that Courage had fled once he learned of his imminent arrest, and you have a pretty damn good case.

The question could be asked, what did Krabbe know that Courage wanted silenced? In comes Larry Slager and his testimony and rental receipt, and you raise the possibility, at least, that Courage had crashed into his wife's car with a towing rig and killed her. Thurber doubted she could pin a murder charge on the man for the old murder, but the suggestion of it now helped with the Krabbe killing and Courage's likely motive. For now, the priority of the current case trumped the old one.

And for the Krabbe murder, she had the bastard nailed. Nailed shut.

It was a perfect case. As soon as she let the word 'perfect' enter her thoughts, she felt a tweak of nerves. Perfect cases worried her because you were expected to close those, send them to the DA with a bow, then watch as the case you built put the criminal away to prison. If you didn't get a guilty verdict on a perfect case, the shit would run all the way back to her.

A call came in on the radio for her.

"Yeah," she said and listened for several seconds to the homicide office receptionist. "Who is she? And she said she saw Courage?"

Thirty minutes later, she merged on to Highway 50, east towards Watt Avenue.

The woman was with a patient when she arrived, so Thurber took a seat in the small waiting room. High profile cases like the Krabbe murder always attracted nut cases and oddballs, generated scores of phone calls to the hotline, and generally created more dust and noise than ten lesser cases combined. It meant sorting through the people who swore they saw Ray Courage at "a bowling alley," "grocery store," "car wash," "Burger King," and dozens of other places, none of which proved either accurate or useful. It meant politely declining the offers of self-proclaimed psychics, clairvoyants, and one guy calling himself a witch doctor, all claiming they were, at the very moment, sensing, channeling, or reading the mind of Ray Courage. Where did these people come from?

Now this Dr. Amanda Bennett, with her doctorate in psychology, no doubt so immersed with nut cases and oddballs of her own that she'd become one herself. Thurber knew that checking out these things was part of the job.

Dr. Bennett's appearance surprised Thurber when the woman walked out of her inner office and approached her. She'd been expecting someone older, likely a recovering hippie, whose interest in psychedelic drugs in the sixties and seventies had found a marginally more productive outlet in psychological therapy. Instead, Dr. Bennett looked like a corporate executive, tall and attractive with a confident and reassuring manner.

"Thank you for coming," she said to Thurber as the two women walked from the reception area into the doctor's private office, sitting

159

down in two armchairs on the far side of the space. "I didn't know if I should call or not. But when I read in the paper this morning about you wanting anyone knowing the whereabouts of Ray Courage to call, I thought it best that I contact you."

"Do you know where he is?"

"No, I'm afraid not. That's one reason I hesitated to call you. I'm probably not going to be of much help to you."

"When you called our office you said that you had seen Mr. Courage. Is that true? And if so, when and where did you see him?"

"I did see him. We spoke for a few minutes. It was here at the office."

"Is he a patient of yours? Is that why he came here?"

"No, not at all. He came asking about whether his wife had once been a client of mine. He said her name was Paula . . ."

"Pamela."

"Yes, Pamela, he called her Pam. Anyway, he explained that she'd died many years ago, and on the day she died she may have been very upset and might have seen a therapist to work things through. See, I was contracted at the time with her company, Crazy Zebra, to see patients through their employee assistance program. Mr. Courage was hoping to find the therapist. I guess to find out his wife's state of mind, or learn something she might have said. I'm not sure exactly what he was hoping to achieve."

Thurber loved this. Courage was doing more digging about the day his wife died. First Krabbe, then Slager, now Dr. Bennett, who would make an impressive witness at a trial. Maybe she actually could build a case for the old murder once she nailed him for Krabbe.

"Was Pam Courage a patient of yours?"

"No. I looked through my files and found nothing about a Pam Courage. I had no referrals from anyone at Crazy Zebra that month, so it wasn't even like she gave an alias. I have some patients who do that. They think there's a stigma with seeing a therapist."

Okay, Thurber reasoned, it would have been better if Pam had been one of Dr. Bennett's patients, but it didn't change things. Courage was still snooping, or in a sense stalking, his wife's last day. Stalking. That word would resonate with a jury. She could work with this.

"Did you two talk about anything else? Did he have other questions?"

"No, not really. He was here about ten minutes, and most of that time was when I was looking through my files."

"I'm probably going to want to come back and get an official statement from you, but just so I can make sure I have things straight for now, when did Mr. Courage come see you?"

"The day before yesterday, the fifteenth."

"That was the day of the murder," Thurber said.

"Yes, that's what I read in the paper. It said that he was a suspect."

"He is. We have a warrant out for his arrest."

"It's kind of scary. Here I was alone with him. I guess he could have killed me if he wanted to."

"I don't think he had any reason to harm you. But I can understand how it might be scary looking back on it." Thurber stood up and shook Dr. Bennett's hands. "This has been very helpful," she said.

"I'm glad I could help."

"Oh, and what time, the day before yesterday, did he come see you?"

"First thing in the morning," Dr. Bennett said without hesitation. "A few minutes after eight. He was waiting at my front door when I arrived for work."

Thurber gave her a forgiving smile. "I think you might have the time wrong. He was home at about eight in the morning." She stopped short of saying *because he was about to shoot Dana Krabbe at that time*.

"Oh, no. I'm sure of it. I have the surveillance tape with him in it if you want to see."

thirty-three

Until she saw the tape showing Ray Courage entering Dr. Bennett's office, Carla Thurber had every reason in the world to believe the man guilty of murder. The tape showed him entering at eight fifteen in the morning. She had Dr. Bennett confirm the veracity of the time stamp by showing her a second tape from a different camera, one inside the building. This one showed Courage, a second time stamp, and a clock on the wall. Eight fifteen. Damn.

She listened to the 911 recording that called in the Krabbe murder. The call came in at eight twenty-one and the caller said he had "just now" heard the shots. Courage would have still been in Bennett's office at eight twenty-one. It was possible the caller's conception of "just now" could have been off a bit. Yet it seemed unlikely that he would have heard anything before eight o'clock—a timeframe that would have allowed Courage to shoot Krabbe and make it to Bennett's office by eight fifteen—and not report it until almost a half hour later. That the call came in anonymously from an untraceable phone added to her unease.

Now she had to go back and see what other holes her case might hold, something she hadn't needed to do before, given the amount of circumstantial evidence against her man.

After knocking on every door on Courage's street, Thurber found a neighbor, three doors down and across the street, who said she'd returned home shortly after leaving for work to get the workout clothes she'd forgotten. "There was a car I'd never seen before parked in front

162

of my house. One of those muscle cars, white with dark tinted windows, but I could see a guy inside through the windshield." She thought it was just before eight o'clock in the morning.

Crap. Not much, but a defense attorney, especially one as good as Mark Scofield, could make hay with it.

Back at her desk, she waited on hold for the Continental Communications manager to retrieve the subpoena she'd faxed over ten minutes earlier.

"Sorry to keep you on hold," the manager said. "This is above my pay grade so I had to get a VP to okay it." Continental offered bundled Internet, cable television, and digital telephone services. Krabbe had been one of their customers. "So again, what was it on this account that you wanted?"

"Three days ago she received a call from the phone number I gave you earlier. We know that already. What I want to see is if that call went to voice mail or if it was answered. Can you do that?"

"Sure. This is the digital age. Hold on a second."

She could hear him working a keyboard. "That call came in at seven twenty-two at night on the thirteenth and lasted fifty-seven seconds."

"Yeah, I know that." Was this guy showing off to her or what?

"It definitely went to voice mail."

"You're sure," Thurber said. "How can you tell?

"I can see it on her account page. There's a link to the message."

"Can you retrieve it and play it for me?"

"I can do better than that. I can e-mail it to you as an audio file."

Thurber played the audio file a second time and then a third. No point in doing so, really. After the first listen, it was clear that Courage was baffled by the content of Krabbe's e-mail, wondering what she could have interpreted as threatening and what she referred as his 'secret.' He ended the message by saying he'd call back the next day to see if they could clear things up. Nothing in his tone or words sounded remotely menacing. He did not invite Krabbe over for a visit the next morning.

Thurber dropped her head into her hands. Never before had a case—especially one as airtight as this—unraveled so quickly and

163

completely. Might as well top it off with some unpleasantness.

Larry Slager did not appear happy to see Lieutenant Carla Thurber pull onto his property. Dirt bag, she thought upon seeing him emerge from the shop.

"Hey, Larry," she said, stepping out of the car and greeting him with a big smile. "How's it going?"

"Okay," he said guardedly. He was wiping his hands on a grimy rag as Thurber approached.

"I was in the area, remembered our terrific conversation from the other day, and thought to myself 'Hey, Larry Slager, Dutiful Citizen, lives and works near here. Think I'll go pay him a visit.'"

"What do you want? I told you everything I know already."

"I figured you were so darn cooperative last time, and what an incredible memory you have by the way, that I bet you can give me even more information."

Slager showed no emotion as he tossed the rag onto the ground in one direction and spit in another. "I'm about to close up shop for the day. So if you don't mind…"

"Well, I do need to ask you a couple of questions, so please stay with me for a couple of minutes. Won't take long." Enough of the warm ups.

"I got about two minutes."

"I understand. A place like this has to set high standards, stay on time, needs to run like a well-oiled machine. With as tight a ship as you run here, I was wondering about a nine thousand five hundred dollar cash deposit you made yesterday at your bank."

"What are you doing looking at my bank account?"

"See, you're a material witness in a homicide. We usually like to see if something might be going on that could, well, influence a witness to say something one way or the other."

"Don't know what you're talking about."

"Where'd that money come from, Larry?" Thurber said, her jaw flexing.

"I … I … I sold some equipment. Guy came in yesterday and gave me cash for an old transmission and some tires."

"Nice you kept it under ten thousand or you would have had to file

Form 8300 with the IRS. So you sold some equipment. Good record keeper like you must have a sales receipt to prove it, right?"

"Just a bunch of old equipment. Didn't need no sales receipt."

"And here you had a rental agreement from thirteen years ago for a truck rental that was way less than ninety-five hundred dollars. I'm really surprised Larry."

"I'm more careful with the rental stuff, that's all." He shrugged.

"You know, about that rental receipt you gave me, I called the company that prints those receipts. Excalibur Printing in Minneapolis. Nice city Minneapolis. Too cold for me, though. Anyway, the guy I talked to at Excalibur said that the rental receipt form you used for Ray Courage was printed three years ago. So I got to thinking to myself, how could a transaction from thirteen years ago have been recorded on a document that's only three years old. So, Larry, tell me how's that possible?"

"Must be some mistake. The printer is wrong."

"No, Larry, not wrong. The guy—who was the company owner by the way—walked me through their system. Even I could figure out the year it was printed. So I repeat, how is it possible?"

"Well … I remember a couple of years ago I transferred some of my old records onto new ones."

"Really, Larry, that's the best you got? You know it's not a good idea to lie to the police."

"I'm not lying. He did come to see me."

Thurber knew that could be true. She'd seen his name on the calendar on Courage's computer. She put her face within inches of Slager's so they were looking at each other eye to eye. "Did he threaten you like you said?"

"Not in so many words, but … but he was … like I said before. He wanted me to keep my mouth shut about the rental."

"Can we drop the nonsense about the rental? That didn't happen, did it?"

"Not saying it did, not saying it didn't. You can't charge me with nothing."

"Who paid you the ninety-five hundred dollars?"

"Guy who bought some equip—"

"Who paid you?"

"I don't know who they were," he said. "They didn't tell me their names or who they were. They just told me to tell you what I told you the other day. That's all. Seemed harmless to me. Didn't mean nothing."

"We're not through," Thurber said, backing away. "I've got to make two phone calls, and while I'm doing that your memory is going to improve. Dramatically. And then you're going to tell me everything about the visit from those two men."

She returned to her car and shook her head, dreading the phone call she hated to make, but had no choice in doing.

"What's up?" her boss, Captain Adam Foster, said answering his cell phone.

"We need to drop all charges against Ray Courage." She spent ten minutes explaining it to Foster before hanging up. If anything, the next phone call would be even worse.

The now-familiar voice of his secretary picked up. "Mark Scofield, please," Thurber said.

thirty-four

After thinking about it some more, Claire decided she didn't want to live in her old home. Too many memories, sure, it was partly that. She didn't remember when her dad died exactly, except for it being the first time she saw her mom cry and the first vivid memory of her childhood. A man and a woman in uniforms had knocked on the front door and came inside. Her mom told her to go to her room so she could talk to them. Then she heard the crying, so she left her room and stood at the end of the hall and saw the uniformed lady hugging her mom. Claire was three or four years old, somewhere in there.

The last time she'd entered the house as a little girl, she'd been told to pack up everything she wanted because she wouldn't be coming back. Her aunt Melissa had said that. Bitch. Never even told her how sorry she felt for Claire losing her mom. Nothing that a normal person would say to an eight-year-old girl who had lost both her parents. Never once did that woman hug her, or tell her she loved her, or even say 'have a nice day.' What kind of person just tells you to pack your stuff and leave the only home you've ever known?

Besides the memories, Claire did not want to live in this house anymore because it moved her backwards. Like the heroin the other day. That had been a mistake, a step back. To achieve her dreams of becoming a singing star, she needed a fresh start in a big city like New York, Los Angeles, or even San Francisco. Tonight would end all the business she had in Sacramento. Then she'd leave. Pack up, tell the agency to rent the place, and clear out the very next day.

For tonight, she told herself to keep her outfit simple and functional, choosing black cotton pants and a black, long-sleeve turtleneck. The black coat hung over a chair in the kitchen. She went over to it and reached into the inside pocket and pulled out the weapon she'd bought yesterday from a guy at the shooting range. She read online that if you wanted to buy a gun without all the legal bullshit, Al's Firing Line was the place to go for a black market weapon.

The clerk at the front had pointed her to a guy drinking a cup of coffee at a table in the snack bar. The man seemed to know his stuff. When he learned that Claire wanted the weapon for personal protection against a stalker, and that she'd never fired a gun before, he suggested a Glock 18C.

"Don't need to be a good shot with one of these babies," he told her. "It's a machine pistol. Shoots nearly twenty rounds in less than two seconds. You just point it at the motherfucker and pull the trigger and you can't miss."

Out on the shooting range, he demonstrated the weapon on a target featuring a human silhouette. "These ain't legal unless you're law enforcement. Bullshit gun control laws. But I'll sell you this one for three thousand dollars. I'll throw in a thousand rounds of ammo for four hundred."

She liked the feel of it, and that it wasn't more than eight inches long, easy for her to hide inside her coat. She liked it even more when she tried it out. The man was right, she couldn't miss a target standing a few feet away.

She put her coat on in the kitchen and practiced pulling the gun from her pocket and firing from her hip. Two hours until her nine o'clock meeting. She looked through the kitchen at the dark street, growing antsier by the second. She wanted to go. Get this done.

She couldn't wait to see Ray Courage's face when she walked up to him and identified herself as Pam1111. She wondered how he would react. She figured if she really had been his wife that he would try to kill her, just as he had really done thirteen years ago. She'd probably driven him half crazy with the idea that he'd failed that night and his wife survived. Claire read all about the accident, just as she had read about how her mom supposedly overdosed on pills and alcohol. Lies.

All of it lies.

When he saw Claire, he'd probably be relieved to know that his wife hadn't really returned to haunt him. Then he'd probably get pissed and try to kill her, just as he had her mother and his own wife.

Claire would not let him get close enough to harm her. If he did approach her, she knew she could pull out the Glock in a couple of seconds. He'd be dead before he knew what hit him. She hoped he wouldn't do that, at least not right away. She wanted to tell him why he needed to be punished for murdering two women so long ago, why she needed to kill him. And then she'd do it.

He, no doubt, thought he'd gotten away with it. He didn't realize that his wife told her therapist about the fight she'd had with her husband that day, and how it had upset her.

"My mom was smarter than you, you son of a bitch." She re-read the note that she'd found clipped to her mom's appointment book, the last thing she had ever written, on the last day of her life:

Patient - Pamela Courage - 916-555-1928
Fight w/husband (Ray, calls him RayRay)
Work issues. Got flustered and rushed out. Fearful. Stalked?
Need to call tomorrow to follow up

Her initial instinct to tell the police was ill-advised. They hadn't done squat. At least she'd called anonymously. No, the police wouldn't help her. They were the ones who said her mom drank herself to death, when her mom hadn't had a drink in more than a year. She lived in the same house as her mom. Even at eight years old she knew for a fact her mom wasn't drinking again. And how stupid were the police to not figure out that Pam Courage and her mom died on the same day! If they'd put any effort into it, they would have figured it out. Just like she had.

She'd avenge her mom. She'd played Ray well. Waiting a week after finding the note to e-mail him on November 11, the anniversary of the murders. That made the impact of the messages even more powerful. The "Pam1111" e-mail address was even more inspired. She smiled at how well she'd done. She felt a familiar warmth and a tingling in her arms and legs. The same sensations she'd felt the night she'd run over the beast man, Uncle Jim. This would be even better, getting to see Ray's face, look him in the eye as she meted out long, overdue justice that would taste so sweet.

Ray, Ray, Ray, Ray, Ray, Ray, Ray— thirteen years and now you pay!

thirty-five

At eight in the evening, I found a spot within the "To The Pioneers" monument in William Land Park. The monument's focal point, a statue of a nineteenth century man sitting on a rock, occupied only a small portion of the commemorative area that included a multi-step waterfall, a two-tiered garden, several stone walls, and four seating enclaves, their semicircular stone benches shielded by trellises and thickets of trees and bushes.

I sat in a corner on one of these benches, my presence masked by the darkness, with a direct view of the statue and the entire couple hundred feet leading up to it from the street. No one could sneak up on me, unless they knew where I sat and approached through the dense brush behind me, a tactic that could not be executed quietly. I removed Pam's picture from my wallet, though the darkness made it impossible to view. Just holding it gave me comfort, and the image of my wife—laughing, eyes aglow—in my mind's eye was clearer than it had become on that faded photograph.

Would I see her tonight? After all these years, had she really returned to me? If so, I reasoned, no matter her state of mind, no matter what induced her to think ill of me, I could get her back. If my tormentor was indeed my Pam, I could make her understand that I loved her and that any presumptions about me she held were mistaken, some misunderstanding or misinterpretation of the truth. My wife would know this once she looked into my eyes, and I into hers.

What if the person who appeared tonight wasn't Pam? I had no

171

real contingency for that because the possibilities of the person's identity seemed infinite. Sure, I could narrow it down some. This someone knew that my wife called me "RayRay." How many people knew that? A dozen? A hundred? This person could be a woman or a man. It could be several people involved in a conspiracy, first to spook me, then to frame me for killing Dana Krabbe. Once again, Yuri Mastrov's name kept elbowing into my thoughts.

No matter the outcome of tonight's meeting, first thing in the morning I would go to Mark Scofield's office and, with him at my side, I would turn myself in. I had almost called him earlier in the day to tell him to expect me the next day, but I couldn't risk anything that might expose me to police detection. I didn't look forward to the long process likely needed to clear myself of the murder. And while doing so enduring the speculation about my guilt by the public, my friends, and my family. I didn't allow myself to contemplate the possibility that the frame up had been so thorough and flawless that I might end up in prison for life.

Dealing with that came tomorrow. Tonight brought its own challenges.

The evening had turned cold. I thrust my hands inside the pouch of the hoodie I'd bought a couple of hours earlier from a Goodwill Store. Across the street, fog hovered over a small lily pond and the several baseball diamonds on the vast field beyond, thickening each minute I sat there. A car passed by slowly on the curved street. I tensed. The car continued on, turning right on to Land Park Drive.

"Hello, RayRay."

I nearly jumped out of my skin at the sound of the woman's voice. She stood twenty feet away, too far for me to see her face in the darkness. Even so, her voice and her bearing told me in a split second that she was not Pam.

"I've been watching you," she said. "Thought you were pretty smart getting here an hour early. Thought you could beat me here, surprise me, and then what? Kill me? But I beat you to it. I've been behind the statue the whole time."

I stood up and started to approach her.

"Uh, uh. Stay right there. This is as close as we're going to get."

The disappointment stung. The part of me hoping and praying that it had been Pam all along crumbled in on itself. I had to adjust to the reality of what my head already told me to be true, but which my heart did not accept.

"You're Pam eleven eleven?"

"Clever boy."

"Why? Why are you doing this?"

"Because you have it coming?"

"Why did you pretend to be my wife? Who are you?"

"Oh, RayRay, this is so long overdue. I wanted to tease you a bit, make you think your wife had come back to seek revenge. And I knew your curiosity would let me keep stringing you along. Finally, you'll get what you deserve. It might not ever have happened if I didn't figure it out."

"Figure what out? And how did you know she called me RayRay."

She laughed and shook her head.

"Where did you get the picture? The one you sent me?"

"Internet. But that doesn't matter now."

I stood there trying to process how things stood. As my eyes continued to adjust to the darkness, I could see the woman was young, early twenties. That meant something.

"You're probably shocked as hell right now, aren't you? I bet for the past thirteen years you thought you were in the clear. That you'd committed two perfect crimes. Perfect *murders*. You were wrong, Ray. My mom saw through you. She was going to bust your ass. Yeah, you killed her, but she showed me the way to find her killer." The words flowed out of her in quick, almost hysterical bursts.

I had managed to ease a little closer to her, though a good fifteen feet remained between us. From this distance I could see her a little better. She was medium height, thin, though I couldn't be sure of that with the coat she wore. Her hair looked dark as the night, in stark contrast to her pale face.

"Look, I don't know what you think you know, but you have it wrong. I didn't kill anybody, especially not my wife. We were in love."

"Hah! That's a lie. I knew you'd lie. I have the proof." Her eyes bulged and she sneered at me after she threw the words at me. "You and your wife fought that day."

I did not interrupt, wanting her to keep talking so I could comprehend what this young woman was talking about and how she'd come to believe me a killer. Looking at her wild expression, the whipsaw changes of cadence in her voice, I knew her connection to reality was, at best, tenuous.

"She came to see my mother for therapy and wrote down what your wife said. She fought with you, Ray! RayRay! Then she got scared at my mother's office because you were stalking her. So she ran."

"Are you Susan Whitehead's daughter? Are you Claire?"

That shocked her for a second, the anger in her face turning to confusion. "Never mind."

I shortened the distance between us to ten feet at most. I thought she might have a weapon concealed somewhere in the bulky coat. If so, I was still too far away to subdue her if she pulled out a gun or a knife. Every nerve in my body fired and I could feel the hair on the back of my neck stand on end. She didn't come here just to talk.

"You're like all men. You hurt your wife. Then you hurt my mom. Killed them both."

"Wait a minute," I said, trying to slow her runaway train of emotions. "What exactly did you see or read that leads you to believe that I did what you say?"

She grinned, twisted, knowing. "I'll tell you exactly what it said. 'Patient Pamela Courage. Fight with husband, Ray. Calls him RayRay. Work issues. Got flustered and rushed out. Fearful. Stalked? Need to call tomorrow to follow up.' That's exactly what my mom wrote that day. So what did you do? Did you kill my mom first or your wife? I want to know!"

"I can see why you might think—"

"Shut up! Answer my question."

I feared provoking her either way. Not answering the question, or again denying my guilt, might fuel her rage. Playing along and pretending to be a killer seemed even more perilous.

"Did you kill Dana Krabbe?" I said, a gambit to change her focus and get an answer I truly needed.

"What?"

"Dana Krabbe. She worked with my wife. Did you kill her?"

"I don't have any idea what you're talking about. I've never heard of her. And *you're* the killer here."

"Maybe you know how I feel now. To be accused of something you didn't do. That note doesn't say anything about me killing anyone. And why would I want to kill your mom?"

"Because she knew about you. She knew about you and your wife. You were planning to kill her and the only one who might have known that was my mom and you couldn't take any chances. *Stop!* That's close enough!"

Inch by inch, I'd managed to work a couple of feet closer. I stopped and showed her my palms in an 'everything's cool here' gesture. For Claire, everything was far from cool, because out of her coat pocket she pulled out a gun.

"Whoa," I said, articulate as hell in the face of a firearm. "Please put that down. We need to talk. I'll keep my distance."

"Answer my question. Who did you kill first?" She held the gun at her hip, barrel pointed at me.

"I talked to your aunt today. Melissa Miller." I wasn't sure if bringing up her unhappy home life would deflect her anger or set it over the top and into a shooting frenzy.

"Crazy-assed bitch. About the only worse person in the entire world was her perverted, rapist husband. The two of them deserved each other." Her eyes seemed to go back to some memory.

"I can help you," I said. "You don't want to shoot me. They'll catch you and you'll end up in jail. Let me help you. After what you've been through—"

"Shut the fuck up! Help me? You'll *help me*? Who says I need any help? What is wrong with you?"

"I was just saying that your aunt and uncle didn't treat you right. That you deserve better."

"No, no, no!" she shouted, stomping her foot. "Shut up! I thought this would be more fun. I'm tired of you. It's time."

She leveled the gun at me. I dove for the ground and rolled twice back towards the bench. Two shots rang out, softer than I'd expected. A quick look back and I saw Claire lying still on the ground. A few seconds passed and she didn't move. I called her name. Nothing.

A bullet ricocheted just above my head on the stone seat of the bench. I sprinted towards Claire, her eyes rolled back in her head, a bullet hole in the middle of her forehead, a mass of blood and human goo pooling around her. I grabbed her gun and ran as another bullet *ka-chinged* behind me.

thirty-six

I ran to the front of the zoo, towards Land Park Drive. A car approached, heading towards Sutterville Road. I stood in the street and tried to hail it down. It swerved into the empty oncoming lane to avoid hitting me, continuing on and away from the lunatic in the middle of the street. A second car approached from farther away, tires squealing, its engine in full high-octane whine. Not good.

Across from the zoo's entrance, Fairy Tale Town had long since closed for the day. I scaled the stone wall on which a smiling and fully put-together Humpty Dumpty waved at anyone venturing by. It had been years since I'd roamed the place, not since Sara was five or six years old. Enough footlights dotted the landscaped paths for me to see my way around. Good for me. Good for my pursuers.

Directly in front of me stood a mini-version of King Arthur's Castle, left of that a faux pirate ship. On the other side of the stone fence, a car screeched to a halt and I heard at least two or three men's voices.

"He's in there," one called out.

"You two follow him in," another commanded. "We'll cover the back."

There was nowhere to hide either inside the castle or in the pirate ship. The uneven flagstone path rendered anything above a jog hazardous as I hurried as best I could past a tollbooth and a small footbridge over a stream of stagnant water, which led me to a restroom. I scrambled inside the restroom, searching the inside of the door with my fingers. A deadbolt. Perfect. I bolted myself inside and tried to get my breath back as my heart pounded and my chest heaved.

A stab of panic. They'd search the entire place. They had all night. Once they found the restroom locked, they would simply shoot off the deadbolt. Unbolting the door, I went back into the night and came upon the Children's Theatre, one of the few structures in the place that was a real building, not a replica from a fairy tale. It might offer a hiding place, with several production rooms, a stage, and a seating area. I tried its three doors. All locked.

From behind I heard the steady footfalls of the two men dispatched to follow me over the wall. Somewhere ahead, at least two more men awaited, though I couldn't know if they did so on the other side of the fence, or if they'd entered the confines of Fairy Tale Town so they could finish me inside. To my right, about a hundred feet away stood a barn, a tall one with a gambrel roof.

"There he is!" A flashlight switched on and found me.

I sprinted for the barn, ascending the long, twisty slide on one end that led up to a second floor barn door. The flashlight fixed on me atop the slide. A shot rang out and a bullet pierced the wood siding next to me. Using the guard railings at the top of the slide, I hoisted myself up and onto the slightly sloped top section of roof. The other end of the barn ended next to the chain link fence at the back of the theme park, a row of pines a foot or two beyond the fence line. I crouched and moved as quickly as I could. My right foot gave way, and I almost tumbled, which would have sent me down the side and over the edge to the ground below. The light caught me again as I reached the end of the barn. I took two deep breaths and leapt with everything I had, slamming into one of the pine trees, hugging it desperately. I tested a branch with my foot to see if it would support me. When it did, I began climbing down until I ran out of footholds and had to make a five-foot drop to the ground below. In the darkness I could not gauge my landing and I tumbled loudly.

"He's outside! He's outside!" The two men following me now started to climb the cyclone fence to continue their pursuit outside the park. Around the corner, several feet away, I heard another commotion. Two more men, already on the outside, turned the corner.

"Got him!" one of them shouted.

I took off into the darkness of the adjacent soccer field. I could not outrun them all night at my age and fitness level. There were four of them, all almost assuredly younger than I. The advantage I did have was that I knew this park. Sara played soccer here. I played golf here. I walked my dog here. The one hundred yard lead on them might be enough if I could get to the golf pro shop. I did. Once there, I opened a gate on the backside of the building where they stored their garbage cans. A few feet later, a stand of trees protected me from view as I continued on. At the pumping station, I climbed the chain link fence and dropped inside. The door into the shed, protecting the pumping equipment from the elements, was unlocked. I ducked inside, shut the door, and went to the window facing back towards the pro shop.

Flashlight beams crisscrossed the patio, the putting green, and cart storage area surrounding the pro shop. The opened gate caught the attention of two of them, as they took a position on either side of it.

"Come out, Courage. It's over." One of the men was talking to the garbage cans. His voice was clear in the otherwise silent night. "Come out now and things will be better for you."

When the men received no response, they simultaneously sprung into shooting positions just outside the opening, their guns pointed as they advanced slowly towards the cans overflowing with garbage. It took a couple of minutes for them to determine I wasn't hiding there. One of them swore loudly, and the rest turned back towards the trees just beyond where they stood.

The other two men swept their flashlight beams out into the vastness of the golf course, acres and acres landscaped with old mature trees and dense underbrush. The time they wasted at the pro shop could have enabled me to head out into that acreage in any direction, my path obscured by the foliage and the darkness.

"Goddammit!" one of them cursed, realizing the enormity of the task to find me now.

"You really fucked this up, Root."

"Shut the fuck up," the man who must have been Root said. He struck his critic hard with the back of his hand, sending the man reeling. "You're the one missed the shot."

They huddled and talked for a few minutes, their conversation inaudible now that the pursuit had ended. They again broke into two pairs, both heading west back towards Fairy Tale Town, the first pair taking the northern route through a parking lot, the second heading south through a picnic area.

For what seemed like two hours, I waited inside the shed. The men did not return. My car was parked about a half mile away at the college. I thought about Claire Miller. She had gotten herself killed over a colossal misreading of a cryptic note. Her blunder had cost Krabbe her life as well. And now maybe mine. The only positive that Claire had achieved—if it could be considered a positive—was raising the specter that Pam's death might not have been accidental. I didn't kill her as Claire had thought, but I was beginning to get an idea of who did.

It occurred to me then that no one must have reported the shots. No sirens wailed to descend on the park. No police helicopters hovered overhead, their searchlights crisscrossing the urban oasis, hunting for a fleeing assassin. Were there more in the small army of men who'd chased me? Some dispatched to clean up the crime scene, the rest to kill me?

I exited the shed, climbed the fence, and started walking the dark expanse of golf course. Under a large oak tree at the edge of the park across from City College, I paused to watch the cars go by, a modest stream of traffic rolling both ways on the four-lane road. Twice now the same white Dodge Challenger cruised by, well under the speed limit. Five minutes later it did so again. About a minute behind the Challenger, a second car—a dark Mercedes sedan—became familiar after its third pass by me. Though not certain, I thought a third car, a Honda CRV, might also be part of the posse circling the park. These guys were persistent. They guessed that I'd remained in the park, my only exit one of the four bordering streets.

If I could cross the well-lit road and make it to the college unseen, I'd be fine, my car safely parked in a lot just past the bookstore. The Challenger passed yet again, giving me sixty seconds to bolt from the tree, cross the four lanes, traverse a narrow patch of lawn in front of the college, and disappear into its outdoor hallways. I reached the edge of the road only to confront an unexpected procession of cars. Five, six, seven cars rolled by before I could enter the street, only to be stuck in the middle of the road as another half-dozen cars traveled in the opposite direction. I looked over and the Mercedes drove towards me. I cut in front of one of the oncoming cars, causing it to screech to a stop, the driver laying on his horn and cursing me.

I made it to the first building and looked back to see the Mercedes sliding into a hard left turn, cross the oncoming lanes, and bound up the sidewalk to the lawn. This late at night the school sat empty, not even a school cop patrolled the dimly-lit campus. I made it to the quad as several shots rang out. They were shooting blindly, maybe a hundred feet behind me as I ran past the cafeteria, past the gym and bookstore, into the parking lot where I found my car. My shaking hand fished in my front pocket and found the car keys.

I dropped them. When I reached down to pick them up, my foot accidentally kicked them underneath the car. There wasn't time to retrieve them.

By now, I'd stopped thinking and had to rely on animal instinct, the instincts of prey cornered by a much more powerful predator. I ran again, now heading across the parking lot towards the football stadium. A rumble and a screech of metal on metal came from the other side of the structure. A sound that gave me hope.

The Challenger entered the parking lot from the north entrance. I hopped over a waist-high fence separating the student and faculty lots. Three, maybe four seconds later, I heard the fence rattle again. They'd scaled the fence just behind me. Rounding the corner of the stadium, I saw the light rail train, the platform empty of passengers.

"Northbound train," said a man's recorded voice from inside the train.

The hiss of the doors starting to close prodded me, and I arrived in time to wedge my hand inside as the doors squeezed shut. A volley of gunfire erupted.

I crouched down, the bullets peppering the side of the train. I pulled hard on one of the doors, springing it open as I leapt inside, rolling onto the floor as the door shut. The train began to move. I went to the window and saw six of them standing in the penumbra of a streetlight, guns dangling at their sides.

November 18

thirty-seven

I rode the light rail all night, changing trains as often as I could to keep my pursuers off track. I managed to doze now and again, getting maybe a couple hours of sleep. At six in the morning, I took the line that delivered me three blocks from Rubia's home. I woke her and, though she pretended to be irritated by the early morning visit, I could see the elation in her face.

Apparently, I was the last person in Sacramento County to learn I'd been cleared of Dana Krabbe's murder. Mark Scofield had called Rubia to tell her the news and ask if she'd seen me. Over eggs, bacon, and toast she filled me in on why Lieutenant Thurber had been compelled to drop the charges.

"I bet that broke her heart," I said.

"Yeah, when she came by the bar to question me about you, I got the feeling she didn't like your ass. Didn't much care for me either since I didn't give her jack. At least now it's over."

"Not exactly." In richly embellished detail, I filled her in on the previous three days' events, starting with my motel escape and culminating in my eluding the gunmen.

"Wow, who are you, Batman?"

"I was thinking more Spiderman, what with the fence thing and the tree and all."

"Nah, any kid can do that. Old man, like you, that's pretty good, though. You're lucky you didn't take a bullet." In two bites she finished off a huge piece of bacon, then chomped down on a piece of sourdough toast. She washed that down with a swallow of coffee.

"I'm glad to see my travails haven't diminished your appetite."

"You know me, Ray. Nothing can diminish my appetite." She drank some more coffee. "So you really think it's Yuri Mastrov?"

"Yes."

"Why? He's a multibillionaire. No offense, but why does he give a rip about you?"

"This is conjecture but—"

"English, please."

I rolled my eyes at her in mock annoyance. "This is a guess based on what I know so far—"

"That's better. Now go on."

"In short, I think he believes I might be able prove he killed Pam," I said.

"Can you?"

"No, but he doesn't know that. I think I can piece together how it might have happened. Dana Krabbe told me Pam was upset the day she died, so much so that she wanted to talk to a psychologist about it. That wasn't really like Pam. She was always even-keeled. But she was under a lot of stress then, and something that day pushed her to the brink."

"And it happened at work, at Mastrov's company?"

"Right. I talked to two of her co-workers in the finance department back then. Jason Upland and Tom Patel. They didn't have a lot of details, but it sounded like Pam disagreed with Mastrov on a financial reporting issue. This was right before they were going to go public with the company. Big money was at stake. From what Patel said, it sounded like they were trying to make it look like the company had more cash than it really did. You know, to boost the stock price. My wife wouldn't sign off on that."

"So he killed her?"

"I'd bet my life on it. Nothing else makes sense."

"Why didn't he just fire her and get a new finance manager?"

"That I don't know. Maybe losing your finance manager right before a public offering can destroy the deal. Maybe Pam told them she had an ethical responsibility to report them to the SEC, or Wall Street, or whoever. Or maybe Mastrov just didn't like anybody telling him no."

"Why'd they kill the shrink, the *chica's* mother?"

"That's the therapist Pam ended up going to that day. They were probably following her. From what Claire said, her mom noted that Pam was scared and thought she might have been stalked. Maybe they found a file and it mentioned more details about what was troubling Pam and it included information about Mastrov. The note didn't say much. Claire said her mom jotted something like 'work issues,' which I doubt would be enough to get her killed. Besides, they didn't even find the note. I guess because it was in her appointment book and not a file. Who knows? I just know that two women dying on the same day right after they'd met couldn't be a coincidence."

Rubia mulled that for a second. "Everything I've heard about Mastrov, he's supposed to be a mean SOB. Rich but mean."

"Claire opened up a can of worms with those e-mails to me and her call to Thurber. Got me snooping around my wife's accident. Somehow Mastrov found out. When I went to see Krabbe, that must have spooked them. She was a direct link to Crazy Zebra and Pam's final day. I'm not sure how they kept tabs on me but they did." A thought crossed my mind and I made a mental note to follow up on it. In all likelihood they'd been tracking my car, and most likely bugged my house and monitored my e-mails. "They couldn't risk me figuring out they killed Pam, and they probably thought Krabbe was too much of a loose end."

"Killing her and framing you got them a two-fer."

"Seems that way to me. Somehow they knew about my meeting Claire last night." Again, I had to conclude they had been accessing my e-mail account.

"Once you were no longer a suspect for Krabbe, then Mastrov knew he had to kill you to take you out of the picture, too," Rubia said, completing my line of logic. "You going to the police with it?"

"No, I have no evidence for any of it. Slager, slime bag that he is, didn't rent a truck to anyone that night. Didn't even rent trucks back then. Krabbe's dead and even what she did know didn't incriminated Mastrov or anyone at his company. All I have is my guesswork."

"Conjecture."

"Exactly."

"What about last night? You saw them kill that girl. They tried to kill you."

"As far as I can tell there is no body. No body, no murder. I couldn't see clear enough in the dark to ID the guys chasing me, let alone tie them to the richest man in Sacramento. Mastrov and his guys are good. I'll give them that."

"You're talking about the guys that killed your wife."

"That's the number one thought in my head at the moment."

"So what are you going to do?"

"I spent seven hours riding light rail thinking about nothing else. You going to be around later?"

Mackey

thirty-eight

Bill Krikorian was a teddy bear of a man, a bit short, a bit stout, a bit gray at the temples, befitting a man who'd worked as a counselor at the same high school for thirty-three years. I considered him a good friend, and I didn't have many of those, someone I'd met in my academic orbit some twenty years before. We shared a love for baseball and academia, two topics that could keep our conversations going for hours on end.

He also loved wine, which is why I brought a bottle of Beringer Private Reserve Cabernet Sauvignon on my visit to The Buckingham School. We greeted each other warmly, months having passed since we'd seen each other face to face.

"For you," I said handing him the bottle of wine. "I didn't bother to wrap it or put it in a gift bag. I figured that would be a waste of time and energy considering it's not likely to make it past eight o'clock tonight."

He surveyed the label and seemed genuinely surprised. "Ray, this is too much."

"No, not at all. I know you like Cabs." The bottle had cost me a hundred and sixty dollars.

"But this is … well it's a special treat. Thank you." We sat down in his small office, little more than a desk, a side table for his computer, a credenza, and the two chairs we sat in. "To what do I owe the honor of your visit?"

"Just in the area," I said.

186

"Just in the area carrying an expensive bottle of Cabernet. You being someone who doesn't drink wine."

"I'm a tad transparent," I said. "I wanted to get your take on the Giants third base situation. What do you think, promote the kid from Triple-A, or trade for the veteran? The radio guys are pushing for the trade."

"You know my view on that. Always build from within the system when you can. Fill in where you have to with free agents, but eighty-percent or more should be homegrown talent. That's the way to build consistency. And in the short and long run, it keeps the payroll more reasonable."

"That's my take, too," I said. "Promote the kid. They have enough bats in the lineup to protect him."

He took another look at the bottle of wine and I could tell he was looking forward to cracking it open tonight.

"How's Olivia?"

"She's doing great. Retired last year. We just celebrated our fortieth anniversary."

"Congratulations. Give her my best."

He asked about Sara and I updated him on all her accomplishments, not at all self-conscious about sounding like the proud father.

"How's the Buckingham team going to be this year?" I said.

"We actually have two or three kids who are on some D-I radars. One kid, a lefty pitcher, might even get drafted. He's got a fastball in the low nineties and a wicked curve."

"I'll have to catch a game or two this season."

There was a short lull in the conversation, which Bill interrupted. "You know I love talking family, and even baseball in November, but I have the feeling you came here for something else." He made a point of patting the bottle of wine with his hand.

"I bring you a student like Demetrio and I have to justify why I came to visit?"

Bill laughed. "Got any more like him?"

"Yeah, his sister.

"We've already got her. Anyone else?"

"Working on it." I decided there was no subtle way to bring up the subject I'd come to discuss. "Elena Mastrov," I said, tossing the name as if anteing in at a poker game.

"What about her?"

"She's a student here, isn't she?"

"She is at that. A senior."

"Is she a good student?"

Bill smiled and set the bottle of wine on his desk. "You know I can't say anything about her academic record. Family Educational Rights Privacy Act. Sorry."

"Ah, good old FERPA. Between HIPPA, FERPA, and all the other federal acronyms, it sure makes it tough for a nosey SOB like me to find out anything."

"Why do you want to know about her?"

"It's got something to do with a case I'm investigating. Her name came up is all."

"Is it important?"

"Actually, it is."

"She wouldn't be in any trouble, would she?"

"I guess that would depend on how things play out," I said.

He started to say something, then stopped himself, recognizing my vague answer was my own way of saying I had my own privacy act.

"I suppose I could talk in general terms as long as I don't say anything specific about her," he said, glancing at the bottle of wine.

"I understand she has a perfect SAT score."

He smiled. "Looks like you don't need me if you have information like that."

"Anybody else score that high?"

"Demetrio came close, with over a 2300, and a girl named Jamie Moore also scored a perfect 2400. But you didn't hear that from me. Elena and Jamie are friends. Tennis players. Both are ranked in the top ten in Northern California for under-eighteen girls."

"Just out of curiosity, when did Jamie get her 2400?"

"It was in December last year," Bill spoke more openly, perhaps because my questions focused more on someone other than the student I'd come calling about. "First time she took it. I remember because she was all done with it. No need to take it again if you get a perfect score. All her classmates were jealous. Most of them had to take it in the spring and then retake it this fall. At a school like this, where the students and parents are ultra-competitive, what you scored on the SAT defines you."

"Where is Elena applying to college?"

"Sorry, I can't tell you. But if you think about what covers the outfield wall at Wrigley, you might give yourself a hint."

"Ivy league."

He held up his hands in a 'who knows?' gesture.

I thanked him for his time and promised to call in the spring so we could catch one of the Buckingham baseball games together.

I still needed to get to Mark Scofield and apologize for the stress I'd put him through by going AWOL, and to pick up my car he'd retrieved from the impound yard. Then I had two calls to make—one to the U.S. Tennis Association's Northern California office, the second to Yuri Mastrov, the man who had killed my wife.

thirty-nine

"Hello, Ray?" Rubia said. "Ray? Spaceship Endurance to Ray Courage. Over."

Your wife dies once, crushing you, burying you so deep, it takes you years to climb out. And only then because not doing so might destroy the other love in your life, the little girl you would do anything to keep from harm, to shower with love. After years go by, it gets better. Not good, but better.

One day, like waking from a dream, you learn your wife is not dead. It was all some mistake. Every coping strategy you used to stave off the pain for those years vanishes. Now you can hope again, now you can feel again, now you can love again.

Hoping that Pam still lived was irrational, as irrational as love itself. The delusion became real to me. Having the delusion of her taken from me hurt almost as much as the first time I lost her. Last time the pain paralyzed me, the sadness turning inward, grief my companion.

This time I felt different. This time the pain triggered an anger inside me that had never been there before. It motivated me. And it scared me. It so consumed me that I didn't know if it would provide an advantage or a handicap in the coming hours.

"Yeah," I said to Rubia.

"About time. I thought we lost you there."

"Sorry. A lot on my mind."

"Gee, really?" she said.

"What's Spaceship Endurance?"

"The spaceship in *Interstellar*? The movie? You know, Matthew McConaughey? Mister Stud Bucket? Come on, Ray, have you been to a movie since they added sound?"

"He's kind of a pretty boy for your taste, isn't he? Aren't you more of a Vin Diesel kinda woman?"

"The things you don't know about me."

We sat in Rubia's tiny kitchen just after four in the afternoon. I couldn't risk going home with Mastrov's men still on the hunt. In all probability my place had been bugged. I'd found the GPS tracker under my car as I'd suspected. My e-mail had to have been hacked by them as well. If they still had the means to track me to Rubia's, I figured they would have already done so. Rubia's home remained off their radar.

I repeated my plan to her for a third time to see if she detected any flaws. Events would happen quickly over the next several hours, and I needed to orchestrate each move and anticipate every possible counter move. I'd satisfied both Rubia and myself, answering her first barrage of questions without a problem. She pressed on.

"What if Mastrov refuses to play along with you?"

"He won't refuse. The man is obviously paranoid. He strikes me as a guy who won't tolerate even a single loose thread. He'll play. I'm sure of it."

"But what if he doesn't."

"Then I'm wrong about him being behind the killing," I said. "And we'll find that out as soon as I call him."

"What did you tell Scofield when you gave him the envelope?"

"I told him not to look inside unless I didn't call him by nine tomorrow morning."

"Guarantees that Mastrov won't have a weapon?"

"We'll be in a public restaurant. He's a well-recognized person. He wouldn't shoot me. We'll get there an hour early to make sure we can watch him come in and that he doesn't have someone undercover inside."

"Upland and Patel's willingness to go on record about the accounting practices at Crazy Zebra?"

"In truth, that's not likely at all. Mastrov won't know that when we meet tonight. He'll know it's a possibility. They're both respected professionals in the financial community. Using their names should be enough to bluff him, at least for tonight."

"What about them? What's keeping Mastrov from killing them to keep them quiet?"

"Their safety is part of the deal I'm putting on the table. He guarantees leaving them alone or I don't live up to my end of the bargain."

We went over the logistics next. I would arrive after Rubia and Cuellar surveyed the parking lot and restaurant to ensure Mastrov had not positioned any of his men there. If any of them showed up after our meeting started, Rubia would text me, and she and Cuellar would move in to back me up.

"Hell, Ray, I think you've got it covered. You're sure you want to do this?"

"Never been surer."

"He's the big, bad wolf, and you're a former school teacher. The odds aren't with you here."

"I don't have much choice. If I don't settle things now, Mastrov's men will kill me as soon as they get the chance."

She gave me a worried look. Despite the plan's thoroughness and our combing over it to check for fatal flaws, Rubia's face told me she had doubts.

"Don't worry," I said. "We've got it covered."

"I don't know. Something just doesn't feel right about it."

"Don't be such a worrywart. It doesn't become you. Let's call the bastard."

For fifteen minutes I waited on hold, contemplating my adversary.

Evil. Mastrov was evil incarnate. Never before had I stared evil in the face. Shrink away or rise to meet it. I shrank in the past, maybe not from evil, but from the unpleasant or the uncomfortable. The depth of Mastrov's depravity, his utter disregard for decency—all driven by what? Money? Power? I couldn't begin to understand the motivations of a man like that.

Evil. You spend your life from childhood on looking for the good, the sunshine, avoiding the dark corners where humanity's darkness dwells, where murder, rape, torture, and epic violence rule.

Our family didn't know it at the time, but evil reached out and grabbed us the day Pam began to work for Yuri Mastrov. That evil grew first infecting my wife's soul then killing her. It continued to grow in the twilight, oblivious to me, until it returned now with redoubled malevolence.

I would conquer evil or I would die. For the first time in my life, I didn't worry about the latter.

"What can I do for you, Mr. Courage," Mastrov said when he finally picked up the phone.

"Why don't we just get to the point of all this and skip all the verbal foreplay? You want me dead. I have something to offer you to make it worth your while not to kill me." I was recording the conversation, though I knew he wouldn't say anything incriminating over the phone.

"Do I know you?"

"Oh, for god's sake. Are you really going play it this way?"

"I had a Pam Courage who worked for me many years ago. Poor woman died in an automobile accident. Tragic, just tragic. Are you related to her?"

I sighed. The son of a bitch wasn't even going to recognize me.

"Here's how it's going to work," I said. "You and I are going to meet at the Pheasant Club Restaurant in West Sacramento at eight o'clock tonight. I've got a table in my name in the back corner. Come alone. It will be just you and me."

"I'm confused, Mr. Courage, why would I want to meet with you tonight? Or meet with you at all for that matter?"

"That will be very clear once we meet. You have a very successful company. You have a beautiful and talented daughter. I don't imagine you would want to risk either one of them when there is no reason to do so."

"Are you threatening my family?" he said. As I hoped, I'd gotten under his skin, the anger in his voice controlled yet unmistakable.

"Not a threat. Just business. I have something that could pose a threat to two of the things you value the most. I'm offering you a way to eliminate those threats. That's all. Very simple really."

"I don't believe you. What could you, a so-called private eye, possibly have that could be a threat to me?"

"Do you really want to do this on the phone? We can if you want. But maybe I'm recording this conversation. Some of the details about your business affairs might prove to be a bit problematic, should they come to light. Besides, I want to look you straight in the eye when we talk. That's something you never seem able to do. You just dispatch your little army of henchmen to do your dirty work. Coward."

"You motherfucker!" he said.

That made me smile. I still had that old communication professor magic in me.

"You have no idea what you're getting yourself into," he continued. "I'll be there tonight. And you'll be sorry to see me."

"Oh, I doubt that," I said. "Oh, and Yuri baby, be sure to bring your checkbook."

I hung up on him and gave Rubia a satisfied smile. "That was fun," I said.

"You were even more annoying than usual."

forty

Never a thriving hub for upscale commerce to begin with, It's My Life's commercial-industrial neighborhood after five o'clock became as abandoned as a bombed-out war zone. The Vietnamese women working at the nail salon piled into an old Camry and drove off. The Mexican mercado's owner and his wife rolled down the metal security door and fastened it with a thick padlock before heading home. The two young Hmong men, who operated the hubcap and tire wholesale store, spent a half hour moving their inventory from their parking lot into the small garage that served as office and warehouse. They were gone by four thirty. And the Goodwill Industries clerk left precisely at five. Even the Korean massage parlor closed down for the day, this part of town so sketchy and off the beaten track that even a horny college student wouldn't risk it for a twenty dollar stress reliever.

Rubia and I sat alone in the IML office feeling secure in our isolation as we prepared to start our plan. Rubia and Cuellar would leave first, as soon as Cuellar arrived. If things looked suspicious at the Pheasant Club, then she would call the IML landline and we would come up with a contingency plan. If everything looked good, she'd call and give me the green light, with the intention of my arriving at the table about an hour before Mastrov. The restaurant would be neutral ground, but I wanted to convey to him, subtly, that I had the upper hand by occupying the table before he did.

I surveyed the IML office space, which could only be described as dismal, consisting of little more than the two battered desks, a

195

threadbare sofa, and the two mismatched armchairs we sat in. The place needed a few thousand dollars and then some.

"What?" Rubia said, observing me.

"Just seeing what a few bucks might do to spruce this place up."

"I'm sorry. My November issue of *Martha Stewart Living* is late."

"What did you use instead, *Larry The Cable Guy's Guide to Interior Design?*"

"I have a limited budget.

"Apparently."

"You know, if I didn't like you so much, I would kick your sorry ass out of here."

"About that, I have little doubt."

"Geez! Has anyone ever told you that you talk like you're in a Shakespeare play when you're nervous?"

"Who says I'm nervous?"

"I do."

"Okay, maybe a little. Okay, maybe a lot." I looked around the room again. "Anyway, if this works out, we'll move you into different digs. Maybe someplace with a gym and space for a tutoring center."

"Wouldn't mind that," she said. "What time you got?"

"Six fifteen."

"Cuellar's late." She tried his cell phone. He did not answer.

"If you want to head over to the restaurant now, I can just tell him to meet you there once he arrives."

"Okay." She rose from the chair and walked to the front door. She paused just as she opened it. "It's going to work out, Ray. It will."

More pep talk than belief, but I appreciated it nonetheless. I nodded and she left.

The dim light from two desk lamps and a floor lamp cast a depressing pall across the room now that Rubia had departed. The past seven days had changed me, unmoored me from the person I had become after fifty-two years, a man defined by his roles—father, husband, college professor, private investigator. A man cast in middle-class values, beliefs, and attitudes. After fifty-two years, some shifts and modifications to my worldview could be considered normal. The foundational shift I now felt developing in me came only in the face of extreme circumstance, so life-altering it could never be reversed, the old Ray Courage forever dead.

Maybe that should have saddened me. After all, it was the old Ray Courage that Pam had fallen in love with, and the person my daughter had come to love and respect. My transformation was so thorough and complete that I didn't care what the old Ray Courage thought or felt. I needed to be someone different to survive in a world run by those like Yuri Mastrov.

Plan or no plan, I couldn't sit there and wait any longer. Arriving a few minutes earlier shouldn't be a problem. Before I reached the door to leave, I was surprised when Rubia opened it and re-entered the office, her face ashen, her eyes pleading forgiveness when they met mine.

Three men followed her in. I recognized Yuri Mastrov from our meeting long ago, and his multiple appearances in the local media. The other two men I did not recognize, though they might have been sent by central casting under the category "thugs."

So much for gaining the upper hand. I tried to hide my surprise, though it was doubtful I succeeded. They didn't display any weapons. All three of them wore suit coats sufficient for hiding firearms.

"Gentlemen," I said, standing up. "I was hoping we could have met at the restaurant. They have excellent deep-fried ravioli. But this worked for me, too. Please sit down. I see that you've met my colleague, Rubia."

They did not heed my invitation to sit, so the five of us remained standing, Rubia to my left, the three men opposite us a few feet away.

"Mr. Courage, first of all I have to say that you are a very ungrateful man," Mastrov said. "As I recall, I paid you well, after your wife's accident, and you choose to thank me by this harassment."

"You mean blood money. And I'm sorry I took it. I wouldn't have if I knew what I do now."

Mastrov fixed me with an icy glare. "What is the nonsense you talked about on the phone earlier?" Mastrov said, getting right to the point.

"By the way," I said. "I found that GPS tracker you put under my car. Clumsy me, I accidentally smashed it with a hammer. Hope you don't mind."

Mastrov stood expressionless, awaiting an answer to his question.

"I also figured you've been hacking into my e-mail account. For thirteen years? Wow, you must really be paranoid about what you did to my wife to be so persistent. If I didn't hate your guts, I'd admire your resolve."

"I asked you a question," Mastrov said.

"Aren't you going to introduce me to your pit bulls here?"

Again, my question received nothing more than a blank stare. I'd forgotten the sheer size of the man, a truly impressive beast, tall, and probably two hundred fifty pounds that looked to be all muscle. His two sidekicks, while not quite as tall, looked equally intimidating. Rubia could hold her own with anybody in a fight, but the two of us would be no match for these three if our conversation blew up into a fight.

"Well, if you're going to be so ill-mannered, then I suppose we should get right to it. You're going to find my offer very generous considering how high the stakes are for you."

Out of the corner of my eye, I could see Rubia inching towards her desk, where I knew she kept a handgun. The problem was that she kept the gun drawer locked. Getting to the drawer, unlocking it, and retrieving a gun seemed to be an unlikely goal under the watchful eyes of the three men. If they frisked her out front, they already knew she'd not been carrying a weapon, something I had insisted on when we conceived our now-abandoned plan.

"So here is my offer, Yuri. Hope you don't mind me calling you Yuri. It's kind of a cute name, warm and fuzzy. Anyway, I will promise not to share, with the authorities, the information about the financial irregularities associated with Crazy Zebra's initial public offering."

"What are you talking about? What irregularities?"

"The sudden infusion of cash from an offshore entity. Russian, I believe. Half a billion dollars to be exact. You deceived your investors by overstating your cash position. My wife wouldn't sign off on the deal, so you killed her."

Mastrov laughed. "That's it? That's why you called me? That's all you've got?" He looked at his two men, who smiled back at him.

Mastrov seemed genuinely relieved. "You've got nothing. That was over ten years ago. The IPO was a huge success. Every investor has made a huge profit on their holdings. So, even if you had any information about this so-called offshore cash—which I highly doubt— my investors wouldn't care. Crazy Zebra's probably the best investment they ever made."

"Maybe they wouldn't care, but the SEC would."

"You've made a huge mistake. The statute of limitations on financial fraud is five years."

"Figured you'd say that," I said. "But dropping a dime to the SEC might just get them to look closer at your current books. Most frauds like you are habitual, so I'm sure they'd find something. Once that hit the news, things could get a bit ugly for you, don't you think?"

"I have nothing to hide. I would welcome the SEC. And once they found nothing wrong, I would sue you for defamation."

"We're not getting anywhere here. You see things one way, I see them another. I guess we'll just have to do what we have to do on this one."

Mastrov shook his head and turned to the man on his right. "Root, I'm going to leave now. Please give me five minutes, then I'd like you to take care of this mess here. Be sure to clean up after you're done." He turned to leave.

"Actually, Yuri, we're not quite done here."

"Yes we are."

"I haven't finished my proposal. I think you'll like this part. It concerns your daughter, Elena."

forty-one

That stopped Mastrov in his tracks. The mere mention of his daughter put him on high alert.

"Yeah, seems she's done very well in the classroom. And that SAT score—twenty-four hundred! Wow!" I nodded, feigning my admiration for the girl. "Too bad she cheated. Didn't even take the test that day. A nice girl named Jamie Moore took it for her. I've got witnesses. The College Board will have signature identification logs that will show Elena's forged signature. Once they compare it to her real signature she'll be exposed. Happens all the time. It would be a shame to lose out on playing tennis at Harvard over a little misunderstanding about, I don't know, ethics."

"You don't know that."

"Oh, I do. And I know what you're thinking right now. That all you have to do is have Larry and Moe here kill me and this will all go away. But you see, I have written down everything I told you and then some. I've got witnesses names and contact information, I have specific dates and events, and so on. I have given it to someone with the instructions that if he doesn't hear from me by nine o'clock tomorrow morning, then he is to take the information to the proper authorities."

"You think you're very clever, don't you?" Mastrov's eyes burned with intensity, no doubt the same fire he showed as a fighter on his way to the world championship. "What are your terms for this information you claim to have?"

"I'm glad we're moving the conversation forward," I said, my tension easing just a bit. "First of all, you don't kill us. I think that goes without saying. And then you deposit ten million dollars into the bank account of the It's My Life organization, which is where we're standing, by the way."

"You have lost your mind. Ten million dollars?" Mastrov scowled.

"Yes, I'm promising not to tell anyone about your financial dealings, or your daughter's SAT scores, for our lives and ten million dollars, ass wipe. The first is for calling off your thugs. The ten million is for killing my wife. If I could prove it, I'd watch them send you to death row. Since I can't, I figure ten million dollars invested in IML would be a fitting tribute to her memory."

"What would prevent you from taking the ten million dollars and then turning around the next day and submitting your alleged information to the authorities?"

"If I send it out after collecting your money, I suspect my life expectancy would be very short. If you kill me later, then the envelope gets sent to the SEC, the College Board, and the police. But if we both play nice, it's a win-win situation."

"You've thought this out quite well, haven't you?" Mastrov said. He smiled and shook his head. "Unfortunately, not quite well enough. You see, Mark Scofield will not be sharing all your wonderful research with anybody. Because he no longer has the envelope you gave him. After he closed the office this afternoon, we went in. Very shoddy security system he has there. Root."

With that, the man he called Root pulled an envelope out of his jacket. He opened it and pulled out the five pages of notes I had put in there just hours before. I was screwed.

"What makes you think that I haven't put a copy in my safe deposit box, and given copies to five other people with the same instructions?"

"I'll take my chances. And you don't own a safety deposit box. You really shouldn't tangle with someone out of your weight class, Mr. Courage. As you are about to see, it ends badly for you."

Through the parted curtains at the front window, I could see movement in the dark parking lot. A glance over at Rubia and I could tell she saw it, too. A few seconds later, someone peered through the window. Cuellar took in the scene inside IML and moved quickly away. Suddenly, our odds improved, especially if the display Cuellar put on at the middle school translated into a similar performance with three armed men. Rubia and I gave each other barely perceptible nods. When Cuellar entered the room to distract them, we'd make a move. My right hand twitched in anticipation of throwing the first punch at Mastrov's blocky face.

The door opened. None of the men moved. Cuellar walked in.

"Cuellar, watch out!" Rubia called out.

Cuellar did not react. Mastrov turned to him and said, "Lobo, you're here just in time. We just finished our business and we were about ready to put a ribbon around it."

"Cuellar?" I said, looking at him for clarification.

His coal black eyes stared back at me. A wry smile crossed his face as he unholstered a gun from underneath his coat and pointed it at me. As he did, Root and the other thug pulled out their guns as well.

"Again, Mr. Courage, you are so much out of your league on this one I'm amazed you survived this long. I commend you for finding the GPS and realizing we've been monitoring your e-mail all these years. Those were precautions to make sure you didn't learn anything harmful to my interests. But you don't think I've built a multibillion dollar company from scratch without being thorough do you?"

"He works for you?" Rubia said. Then turning to Cuellar she said, "You bastard."

"So much for the romance of the century," I said, but I don't think she heard me.

"Yes, Lobo works for me," Mastrov said. "He's been my head of security almost since the very beginning."

"Wait a minute," I said to Cuellar. "If you work for Mastrov, why didn't you kill me at the motel the other day?"

"Not that I owe you an explanation, but I will answer that," Mastrov said. "If you turned up dead, or permanently missing—which the police would probably treat as the same thing—they would have begun digging deeper. That could possibly have led them back to me. Maybe not a high possibility but a possibility. We knew you were planning to turn yourself in after the meeting with the girl. Better to keep you alive and in custody. You don't think the police showing up at your motel was a coincidence? Lobo called them. And how do you think we knew you'd be in this dump?"

"Hey!" Rubia protested. Mastrov didn't bother to look at her.

"Once you were in custody, the police would be satisfied that they had the killer of the unfortunate Ms. Krabbe," he continued. "And then maybe they'd spend the rest of their efforts trying to build a case against you for killing your wife."

"That didn't work out did it?" I said. "Your frame job fell apart."

Mastrov shot a look at Lobo, then Root. "The only important thing is that everything will be taken care of tonight, and I can go back to running my company."

"Which one of you bastards killed my wife? You at least owe me that."

Cuellar looked at Mastrov, who gave him a nod. "I did," he said. "Root and I handled that operation. I did the driving. Root set the wreck on fire. Team effort."

The smoldering fire inside me began to grow. Somehow I managed to ask another question without flying into an uncontrolled rage. "Why was she in Clarksburg?"

"Shit, I don't know. I was all set to kill the bitch in the parking lot at the shrink's office before she got to her car. But that other bitch, the shrink, was looking out her window, watching your wife walk to her car. She saw me in the truck and wrote down the license. That's why we killed her, not because of anything your wife told her. Your wife just started driving all over the place. Finally, in Clarksburg, she decided to make a U-turn. I rammed her and Root did the rest."

"Satisfied, Mr. Courage?" Mastrov asked. "Your wife got what she deserved. If she had her way, Crazy Zebra would be a two-bit operation instead of a multinational power. Good night. Lobo, you know what to do."

Mastrov turned to leave, all heads in the room watching as the big man strode to the door. As they did so, I made my move, reaching into my back pocket, extracting Claire's machine pistol. In less than five seconds, I swept the room with a volley of nine millimeter bullets, and all four men crumpled to the floor.

I waited for the lingering smoke from the gunfire to clear, watching intently to see if any of them moved. No one did. The gunpowder smelled sweet, almost soothing, as I felt my breath slow and my heartbeat return to normal. Rubia and I stood in that abject silence, our ears ringing from the explosions, for what seemed like a full minute before either of us spoke.

"Damn, Ray, I thought you didn't believe in guns."

"Sometimes you have to make an exception."

January 2

epilogue

The plane touched down at Sacramento International about three in the afternoon. Sara and I had said our goodbyes in Houston, where she changed planes for Los Angeles, and I boarded mine for Sacramento. We had decided to spend the holidays in Cancun, the recent events diminishing my taste for a traditional cheery Christmas. It was a great trip. Seven days with my daughter, seven days away from the craziness.

The killings dominated the news every day through Thanksgiving, dwindling to a story a week after that, until the buzz finally died around Christmas Eve, the day of my departure for Mexico. After reading the West Sacramento PD's report, the Yolo County Prosecutor's Office found insufficient evidence to charge me for homicide, my actions ruled justifiable. They did file charges against me for possession of an illegal firearm. Turned out the Glock 18C, a fully automatic machine pistol, was legal only for law enforcement. Mark Scofield made the case for how I'd come to acquire the weapon, and the DA eventually dropped the charges two weeks later. By then, public opinion had begun to turn in my favor, and I went from being a "savage gunman bent on revenging his wife's death" to a "valiant defender who saved the life of an inner-city community leader." I didn't care how they wanted to characterize me. I knew the truth.

Rubia picked me up at the airport curb. I tossed my bag in the trunk and buckled into the passenger seat.

"Good trip?" she said.

"Great."

"You okay?"

"Yeah."

We didn't say anything more until she merged onto I-5 and we started back towards Sacramento, just ahead of the rush hour commute.

"Demetrio heard back from Occidental," she said.

"And?"

"He's in. Full ride. He told them he's coming. You said something that made sense to that boy."

"I have my moments." My heart swelled, as if Demetrio was my own son. I made a mental note to call him as soon as I was back at the house.

"Did you read anything about Crazy Zebra while you were in Mexico?"

"Nope. Avoided television, newspapers, and the Internet."

"Turns out he was already being looked at by the Securities and Exchange Commission. Not for the IPO thing, but for shady deals he did last year. The attorney general said yesterday that they would be filing charges next week."

I thought about that and hoped Crazy Zebra would get punished for breaking the law. But I wanted the company to survive. They employed a lot of people, they pumped a lot of money into the local economy. Maybe now that Mastrov was dead, the company could reinvent itself into one that didn't need to break rules. Or kill its employees.

"Yeah, all kinds of crap is coming out on good old Yuri. Now that he's dead, people aren't afraid to talk. MMA officials told ESPN that he bribed referees to fix his matches back in his fighting days. His business competitors claim he used intimidation to win deals, and a couple of them even produced surveillance equipment that Mastrov supposedly put in their homes and offices. His reputation is shot."

"Breaks my heart."

"The *Bee* did an in-depth story on the other three guys. They were all ex-MMA fighters. None of them fought for the sport of it. They were just a bunch of psychopaths who liked to beat the crap out of people. They all had priors for assault and battery."

"Did they have families?" I said. That question had nagged me while I was away. I didn't want to kill someone's father. I even felt some pain for Mastrov's daughter. She hadn't chosen her father.

"Don't think they were the marrying type. And no kids or nothing. Mastrov kept them on call twenty-four-seven, so doubt they had much romance going on."

It had all started with that poor, unhinged girl finding her mother's note. She set in motion a firestorm that killed her and left five others dead. On the flip side, if she hadn't done so, I never would have known Pam had been murdered. Or, bring to justice the men who killed her.

"Did Claire's body ever turn up?" I asked.

"Nope. Just gone."

I pondered that for a second, how her life had spiraled out of control once Mastrov's men had killed her mother. So many tragedies began on that eventful November day, so many years ago.

"I wish I'd gotten that ten million dollars for you," I said.

"Did you really think he'd go for your deal?"

"I was hoping we had a fifty-fifty chance. I figured if he didn't go for it, he'd try to take me down either before the meeting or right afterwards when I was driving home or at home. I didn't see him coming to IML. And I sure didn't see Cuellar being a spy."

"And you checked his references, too."

"I fell for the oldest trick in the book on that. He gave me a name and number of somebody inside Crazy Zebra pretending to be the security company Cuellar worked for. He fooled me."

"He was a good-looking spy, I will say that," Rubia said, shaking her head.

"Looked like John Stamos."

"Yep."

She pulled into my driveway behind my car. I got out, retrieved my bag from the trunk, and went to the driver's side window to thank her for the ride. She had a smile on her face and was shaking her head.

"What?" I said.

"I can't get over that night. You and that gun."

"I almost threw it in the river that morning," I said. "About half-way there I changed my mind. Might doesn't make right, but I got to thinking about what you said that time in the bar, you know about being a live ex-felon with a gun than a dead ex-felon without one. Pretty damn good logic."

"About time you started listening to me," she said. "Why didn't you use it the night before in the park—when all those guys were chasing you?"

"I don't know. I hadn't made up my mind whether to use it or not. I might have, if they came after me in the pumping shed. Who knows?"

Rubia put the car into reverse and started to ease out of the driveway. I started for the house, fishing for the keys in my bag.

"Hey," Rubia called out, leaning out of the window. She'd stopped before the back of her car had reached the street. "How'd you learn to shoot that thing, anyway?"

"Internet."

"What?"

"YouTube."

After she finished laughing at the idea of a boring middle-aged man learning to use a lethal weapon on a medium known more for cat antics and silly GoPro videos, she asked me a final question. "Now that you've gone all Jax Teller on me, are you going to start packing from now on?"

"I don't know. We'll have to see.

About the Author

Scott Mackey lives in Northern California, where he writes both fiction and non-fiction His Ray Courage Mystery books have received international acclaim. Leann more about these books and the others he has written at www. r.scottmakey.com.

Follow him:
Twitter: smackey17
Facebook: Facebook.com/rscottmackey
Goodreads: http://bit.ly/1tMtfF8
Web: www.rscottmackey.com

More Ray Courage ...
Available now on Amazon and other online retailers

Courage Begins
A Ray Courage Novella

Former college professor Ray Courage starts a new career as a private investigator and tries to crack an unsolved murder. In this prequel to *Courage Matters*, Ray Courage begins his private investigation career, displaying the skills, abilities and sense of humor that have made him a fan favorite around the world.

Courage Matters

The first book in the series that's been called the "Breaking Bad" of the private eye genre. Rookie Private Investigator Ray Courage is asked by "Stockbroker to the Stars" Lionel Stroud to investigate an employee who's been acting suspiciously. Ray soon learns that not everything is as it appears at Stroud's firm. When his investigation uncovers a possible Ponzi Scheme orchestrated by Stroud himself, two people are murdered and Ray becomes Suspect Number One. Ray needs to find answers fast to avoid prison ... or death at the hands of the killer. Complicating his efforts are threats from a Mexican drug lord, hostility from a millionaire with a penchant for strippers, harassment from a cop bent on putting Ray away for life, and a rekindled love affair with Stroud's daughter.

www.ingramcontent.com/pod-product-compliance
Lightning Source LLC
Chambersburg PA
CBHW021033130626
46552CB00005B/1821